KREEPY KLOWNS
OF
KALAMAZOO

Here's what readers from around the country are saying about Johnathan Rand's *AMERICAN CHILLERS:*

"Our whole class just finished reading 'Poisonous Pythons Paralyze Pennsylvania, and it was GREAT!"
-Trent J., age 11, Pennsylvania

"I finished reading "Dangerous Dolls of Delaware in just three days! It creeped me out!
-Brittany K., age 9, Ohio

"My teacher read GHOST IN THE GRAVEYARD to us. I loved it! I can't wait to read GHOST IN THE GRAND!"
-Nicholas H., age 8, Arizona

"My brother got in trouble for reading your book after he was supposed to go to bed. He says it's your fault, because your books are so good. But he's not mad at you or anything."
-Ariel C., age 10, South Carolina

"I just finished ALIEN ANDROIDS ASSAULT ARIZONA, and it was really great!
-Tyler F., age 9, Michigan

"American Chillers is my favorite series! Can you write them faster so I don't have to wait for the next one? Thank you."
-Alex W., age 8, Washington, D.C.

"I can't stop reading AMERICAN CHILLERS! I've read every one twice, and I'm going to read them again!"
-Emily T., age 12, Wisconsin

"Our whole class listened to CREEPY CAMPFIRE
CHILLERS with the lights out. It was really spooky!"
-Erin J., age 12, Georgia

"When you write a book about Oklahoma, write it about my
city. I've lived here all my life, and it's a freaky place."
-Justin P., age 11, Oklahoma

"When you came to our school, you said that all of your books
are true stories. I don't believe you, but I LOVE your books,
anyway!"
-Anthony H., age 11, Ohio

"I really liked NEW YORK NINJAS! I'm going to get all of
your books!"
-Chandler L., age 10, New York

"Every night I read your books in bed with a flashlight. You
write really creepy stories!"
-Skylar P., age 8, Michigan

"My teacher let me borrow INVISIBLE IGUANAS OF
ILLINOIS, and I just finished it! It was really, really great!"
-Greg R., age 11, Virginia

"I went to your website and saw your dogs. They are really
cute. Why don't you write a book about them?"
-Laura L., age 10, Arkansas

"DANGEROUS DOLLS OF DELAWARE was so scary that I
couldn't read it at night. Then I had a bad dream. That book
was super-freaky!"
-Sean F., age 9, Delaware

"I have every single book in the CHILLERS series, and I love them!"

-*Mike W., age 11, Michigan*

"Your books rock!"

-*Darrell D ., age 10, Minnesota*

"My friend let me borrow one of your books, and now I can't stop! So far, my favorite is WISCONSIN WEREWOLVES. That was a great book!"

-*Riley S., age 12, Oregon*

"I read your books every single day. They're COOL!"

-*Katie M., age 12, Michigan*

"I just found out that the #14 book is called CREEPY CONDORS OF CALIFORNIA. That's where I live! I can't wait for this book!"

-*Emilio H., age 10, California*

"I have every single book that you've written, and I can't decide which one I love the most! Keep writing!"

-*Jenna S., age 9, Kentucky*

"I love to read your books! My brother does, too!"

-*Joey B., age 12, Missouri*

"I got IRON INSECTS INVADE INDIANA for my birthday, and it's AWESOME!"

-*Colin T., age 10, Indiana*

Don't miss these exciting, action-packed books by Johnathan Rand:

Michigan Chillers:
#1: Mayhem on Mackinac Island
#2: Terror Stalks Traverse City
#3: Poltergeists of Petoskey
#4: Aliens Attack Alpena
#5: Gargoyles of Gaylord
#6: Strange Spirits of St. Ignace
#7: Kreepy Klowns of Kalamazoo
#8: Dinosaurs Destroy Detroit
#9: Sinister Spiders of Saginaw
#10: Mackinaw City Mummies
#11: Great Lakes Ghost Ship
#12: AuSable Alligators
#13: Gruesome Ghouls of Grand Rapids

Freddie Fernortner, Fearless First Grader:

#1: The Fantastic Flying Bicycle
#2: The Super-Scary Night Thingy
#3: A Haunting We Will Go
#4: Freddie's Dog Walking Service
#5: The Big Box Fort
#6: Mr. Chewy's Big Adventure
#7: The Magical Wading Pool

American Chillers:
#1: The Michigan Mega-Monsters
#2: Ogres of Ohio
#3: Florida Fog Phantoms
#4: New York Ninjas
#5: Terrible Tractors of Texas
#6: Invisible Iguanas of Illinois
#7: Wisconsin Werewolves
#8: Minnesota Mall Mannequins
#9: Iron Insects Invade Indiana
#10: Missouri Madhouse
#11: Poisonous Pythons Paralyze Pennsylvania
#12: Dangerous Dolls of Delaware
#13: Virtual Vampires of Vermont
#14: Creepy Condors of California
#15: Nebraska Nightcrawlers
#16: Alien Androids Assault Arizona
#17: South Carolina Sea Creatures
#18: Washington Wax Museum
#19: North Dakota Night Dragons

Adventure Club series:
#1: Ghost in the Graveyard
#2: Ghost in the Grand
#3: The Haunted Schoolhouse

www.americanchillers.com

Johnathan Rand's

MICHIGAN CHILLERS

#7: Kreepy Klowns of Kalamazoo

An AudioCraft Publishing, Inc. book

This book is a work of fiction. Names, places, characters and incidents are used fictitiously, or are products of the author's very active imagination.

Book storage and warehouses provided by Chillermania!©
Indian River, Michigan

Warehouse security provided by:
Lily Munster and Scooby-Boo

Michigan Chillers #7: Kreepy Klowns of Kalamazoo
ISBN 13-digit: 978-1-893699-13-7

Librarians/Media Specialists:
PCIP/MARC records available at www.americanchillers.com

Cover illustration by Dwayne Harris
Cover layout and design by Sue Harring

Printed in USA

Kreepy Klowns
of
Kalamazoo

VISIT CHILLERMANIA!

WORLD HEADQUARTERS FOR BOOKS BY JOHNATHAN RAND!

CHILLERMANIA!

**I-75 Exit 313
then south
1 mile!**

Visit the HOME for books by Johnathan Rand! Featuring books, hats, shirts, bookmarks and other cool stuff not available anywhere else in the world! Plus, watch the American Chillers website for news of special events and signings at *CHILLERMANIA!* with author Johnathan Rand! Located in northern lower Michigan, on I-75! Take exit 313 . . . then south 1 mile! For more info, call (231) 238-0338. And be afraid! Be veeeery afraaaaaaiiiid . . . .

I've always loved carnivals. *Always.* Ferris wheels, games, the smell of nachos and hot dogs, and the excited shouts and shrieks that fill the air on a hot summer day. I love everything about carnivals.

Except the clowns.

Oh, I used to like clowns. I thought they were kind of funny the way they were always goofing off and squirting everyone with water. I thought clowns were fun.

Not anymore. Not after what I just went

7

through.

I'm Kayleigh. Kayleigh Fisher. I'm eleven, but I'll be twelve really soon. I have a brother named Andy, but I usually don't admit it. He's a goof. Not always, but most of the time. He's a year younger than me, and when he's not acting like a complete goof-off, we hang out together.

We live in Kalamazoo, Michigan, which is a city that began as a fur trading post in the 1700s. In 1831, the town was first called 'Bronson' after Titus Bronson, one of the first settlers. It was renamed 'Kalamazoo' in 1837, which comes from the Potawatomi Indian expression 'Kikalamazoo,' which means 'the rapids at the river crossing'.

If you ever come to Kalamazoo, you're bound to see billboards on the side of the highway that say 'Kalamazoo . . . Sounds Like Fun.'

That's true. We have a lot of fun in Kalamazoo.

Until the carnival came to town. Until the Klowns showed up. Yes, that's 'Klowns' with a 'K'. Soon, you'll know why its spelled like that.

The big, colorful tents seemed to arrive overnight. Within one single day, the Arcadia Festival Site had been turned into a huge gallery of fun. Flyers had been hung up all over the city talking about carnival week. And the carnival was going to open on the day of my birthday! What fun. My friends and I had been saving money for over a month. We couldn't wait.

One morning when I went outside, I saw a line of big semi-trucks driving by. They were all different colors, and on the sides of the trailers, colorful carnival scenes had been painted.

Seeing them arrive, my blood started pumping. *They're here!* I thought. *They're finally here!*

As the semi-trucks rolled on past, I stood on the sidewalk and waved. Some of them honked their horns as they went by. My blood pumped harder and I got more and more excited with every arriving truck — until I saw who — or what — was driving them.

They were circus clowns! Circus clowns were driving the semi-trucks. They all had white face-paint and different colored hair. Some clowns had orange hair, some had green or yellow. They looked silly.

But there was something wrong with these clowns. I couldn't put my finger on it, but these clowns just didn't look . . . well . . . *normal.* These clowns looked scary. Scary . . . and *mean.*

They all waved at me as they headed for the festival site, but I stopped waving when one of them looked at me. He smiled, but it just didn't seem to be a happy smile. The clown looked like he was angry.

Oh, he was smiling, all right. But he still looked angry. His eyes were big and round, and he was glaring at me. He looked spooky.

The convoy finally passed by, and I threw away my suspicious thoughts.

Sheesh, Kayleigh, I thought. *Don't be ridiculous. They're circus clowns. Circus clowns are supposed to make you happy.*

I ran back to the house and pushed away my thoughts about crazy clowns. After all, the carnival was in town! It wouldn't be long now. Soon, the air would be filled with the delicious aroma of cotton candy, elephant ears, and popcorn. Kids would be laughing and screaming as they whirled about on the dazzling rides. Bells would ring and happy calliope music would drift across the city. For the next week, my friends, my brother and I would almost *live* at the carnival. The next week would be nothing but nonstop fun.

Or so I thought.

Today was Friday. Tomorrow was my birthday. And tomorrow, the carnival would open.

The nightmare was about to begin

The next morning, my brother woke me up. In the summer, I like to sleep in late. *Really* late. I like to get up right around the crack of noon.

"Happy birthday, Kayleigh!" he shouted from the doorway of my bedroom. "It's almost eleven! Come on! The carnival will be open in an hour!"

He didn't have to tell me twice. I ran a brush through my dark brown hair and got dressed. In less than ten minutes we had both polished off a bowl of *Cap'n Crunch* and were out the door.

We were off and on our way. The carnival was in town! What fun. I'm not sure what I liked better: the carnival, or my birthday.

Hooray! I was twelve. Almost a teenager. *Almost.*

As soon as we rounded our block, we could see the Arcadia Festival Site in the distance. The site is not too far from where we live, and the carnival was being held there this year. Striped tents and brightly colored rides jutted up into the blue sky like wide, fat skyscrapers. Nothing was moving yet, since the carnival didn't officially open till noon.

Andy and I walked quickly along the sidewalk, almost breaking into a run. Mom and Dad had given me ten dollars for my birthday so I'd have money for the rides, and I had stuffed the money into the pocket of my jeans. I had a ten-dollar bill, a few one-dollar bills from my bank, and a bunch of quarters. The quarters jingled as I walked.

Finally, we made it to Arcadia. A tall, wire fence went around the whole carnival area, and the main gate was still closed. There was already a line of people waiting to get in.

I looked at my watch. It was 11:30. We still had another half hour before the carnival would open.

We stood in line and waited for a few minutes.

More and more people began to arrive, and we saw a few of our friends. Families brought their children, boys brought their girlfriends, girls brought their boyfriends. A lot of people were all waiting to be the first inside.

"Hey Kayleigh," Andy suddenly whispered. He spoke quietly so no one else nearby could hear him. *"I think I know a place around back where we could see what's going on. Wanna go check it out?"*

"You mean sneak into the carnival?!?!" I said. That was not something I wanted to do.

"Of course not!" he whispered. *"But the tents are right by the fence! We can get real close to the rides and the tents and see what's going on before anyone else."*

I have to admit, that sounded fun. But we'd lose our place in line. Nevertheless, I agreed to go with him. It would be fun to see everything close up, and before anyone else.

We stepped out of line and followed the fence as it wound around the big field. Tents and rides towered above us, just on the other side of the fence. We were so close, we could have reached out and touched some of the steel beams that held up the rides.

Soon, we came to a tent that had been set up right next to the fence. It was red and white striped, and it was right near the rear entrance of the festival site. This was the entrance that was used by the semi-trucks to unload all of their equipment. It was a private entrance, to be used by the carnival workers only.

And the gate was open!

Did we dare?

No, we shouldn't. We shouldn't, and we wouldn't. Sneaking into the carnival would get us into a lot of trouble.

We stopped walking and looked around. Suddenly a clown came into view! He was walking between two trucks, then he turned and went into a tent.

"Andy," I whispered, raising my arm. *"Look at that tent."*

Andy looked to where I was pointing. The clown had gone through the opening of the tent and was no longer in sight. Above the opening of the tent was a big, hand-painted sign that read:

KLOWNS ONLY - ALL OTHERS KEEP OUT

Someone had better give the clowns some spelling lessons. 'Clowns' is supposed to be spelled with the letter C, not a K.

"That must be where they put their make-up on," Andy said. He turned his head and shot me a sneaky grin. "Wanna go see how the clowns put on their make-up?" he asked.

That would be cool!

But no. We'd have to go through the rear entrance, and we'd get in trouble for sure. And besides . . . I suddenly remembered seeing the clowns yesterday, and the strange looks they all had on their faces. Now I wasn't sure if I wanted to see the clowns, after all.

"Look over there," Andy said, pointing. "There's a tear in the side of the tent! It's right by the fence! We can walk over there and peek through from this side of the fence! We don't even have to sneak inside!"

I was going to say no, that we should just go back and wait in line. But when Andy started walking along the fence toward the tent, I followed.

After all . . . we *were* on the other side of the fence. We weren't doing anything wrong. How could we get into trouble?

We walked quietly to where the rip in the tent was. The tear was only about six inches long, but it was wide enough to see through. I leaned forward, my face almost pressing against the mesh wire fence.

I was peering through the rip in the canvas when a movement close by, from inside, caught my attention.

It was a shadow. The looming shadow of a clown against the canvas tent. It was dark, and I could clearly see his form as he moved.

He stopped just a few feet from where we were. All we could see was his silhouette, but it was easy to see all of his features: his arms, his legs, his head, and his curly hair.

But what was in his hand almost made me scream in horror.

The clown was holding a knife!

3

We stayed as still as we could. I was too afraid to even breathe. I thought that if I took a breath, the clown would hear me. My heart was doing flip-flops in my chest, and I was almost certain that the clown could hear it.

Had the clown spotted us? Had he heard us? He was right near the edge of the tent, gripping the knife tightly in his hand. It looked like he was staring right at us. Maybe he could see our shadows like we could see his shadow.

Right beside me, Andy was motionless. His eyes were fixed on the huge clown shadow only a few feet from us. Neither of us moved.

Then the clown began walking away from the side of the tent. Whew! He hadn't seen us, after all.

Andy leaned forward and peered through the rip in the tent.

"For gosh sakes," he whispered quietly. I could hear the relief in his voice. *"The clown is holding a butter knife! I think he's making a sandwich!"*

I almost started to laugh. *Of course,* I thought. *That's all it was. A butter knife.* I felt silly, thinking that it could have been anything else.

I was relieved, but I still felt uneasy. I couldn't put my finger on it, but the clowns made me nervous. I didn't like the way they looked at me yesterday. I know it sounds crazy, but something told me that I needed to watch out for the clowns.

These clowns, anyway.

I glanced down at my watch. It was 11:55.

"Come on!" I urged Andy. "It's almost time to go inside!"

Reluctantly, he drew away from the fence and stood up. We walked back to the main entrance where a huge crowd of people had gathered. Kids were screaming and laughing, parents were chattering, and smiles were everywhere. We had to get in the back of the line, but I didn't care. I was too excited.

Suddenly, carnival music filled the air. Rides began to squeak and move, slowly at first, then faster. The air was electric and filled with excitement. The crowd around us let out a cheer, and a wave of applause swept through. Andy and I clapped our hands. The roar of applause and cheering was deafening.

The gates opened up, and the crowd began to move slowly forward.

The carnival was opening! The carnival was opening, and there were hundreds — even thousands — of people coming. They were coming to ride the rides and play the games. They were coming to gorge themselves on hot dogs and candy and popcorn and all kinds of scrumptious food. They were coming to have fun, just like we were.

Of course, the clowns had other plans.

4

The line moved quickly, and soon we were at the gate. I dug into my pocket for my money to buy tickets.

When I looked up and saw the clown, I gasped. Clowns were selling tickets! I hadn't seen them before, but there were five or six of them. They sat in ticket booths and sold tickets to people. They looked like the same clowns that were driving the semi-trucks yesterday.

Andy was behind me. "Come on," he prodded. "You're holding up the line."

But I couldn't move. I just stared at the clown. I stared at the clown, and the clown stared back at me. He didn't say anything. He didn't move. He just gazed at me with cold, dark eyes.

And his *smile.*

He was smiling, but it didn't look like a happy smile. It was more of a sneer, like he was all smug and had something to hide. I didn't like the way he looked at all.

Then I noticed something else. *All of the other clowns had the same, strange look on their faces.* They were smiling, but, they all had this cold, dead stare as they took money and exchanged tickets.

"Kayleigh," Andy persisted from behind me. He nudged my shoulder. "Come on! Give him your money!"

I managed to reach out and hand my money to the clown, but I snapped my arm back quickly so I wouldn't touch his hand. He never took his eyes off of mine while he pulled out a strip of yellow tickets and handed them back to me.

I reached out to take the tickets—and he grabbed my wrist!

I would have screamed, but my breath was gone. I couldn't even get my mouth open. I was horrified. The clown's grasp on my wrist was tight and firm. He had wiry, strong hands, and I don't think I could have struggled free if I tried.

The clown leaned closer. I could feel his hand pulling on my arm, pulling me closer, pulling me toward him.

"Enjoy the rides," he wheezed. *"Enjoy the rides . . . ."* His voice was low and gruff, like an animal's growl. His smile grew wider, exposing crooked, yellow teeth. His grip loosened, and I finally yanked my hand from his grasp. I spun and walked hurriedly past Andy and stopped a few feet away.

"What's up with you?" Andy turned and asked me. Then he turned back around and faced the ticket window, handing the clown his money. In a moment, he was stuffing the wad of tickets into his pocket. He strode over to me.

"Didn't you notice anything different about that clown?" I asked him. He turned and looked back at the ticket booth, then turned and faced me. He had a dumbfounded look on his face.

"No," he replied, shaking his head. "Like, what?"

"I don't know," I answered nervously. "But he just didn't seem . . . well, you know . . . *normal.*"

"He's a circus clown, Kayleigh," Andy snickered. "He's not *supposed* to be normal."

23

"Yeah, but—"

"Let's go," he interrupted, turning his attention to the rides that were whirling about. He started walking toward the colorful midway.

I couldn't help but take one more glance at the strange clown in the ticket booth. It was like I could sense him watching me, glaring at me from his chair. I turned to look at him, to prove to myself that he *wasn't* looking at me.

But he was!

He was staring at me with that same, awful grin.

And his mouth was moving! He wasn't speaking, not out loud anyway. But just the same, I could understand him. I watched his lips move, and I could understand what he was saying.

Enjoy the rides, he mouthed. *Enjoy the rides . . . .*

I turned and ran as fast as I could, bumping into people as I tried to catch up with Andy. The clown's voice kept rolling through my head.

Enjoy the rides, it repeated, over and over and over in that deep, throaty growl. *Enjoy the rides . . . .*

Something was very, very wrong at the carnival. *Very* wrong. Why I stayed, I'll never know. I think it was because that deep down, I was hoping I was mistaken. I was hoping that the dark feeling I had, the feeling that was balled up in my gut like a knot, was nothing but my own imagination running away with me.

I was hoping that I was wrong about the clowns.

But I wasn't wrong—and I knew it. And it wasn't going to take very long to find out that my worst fears were about to come true.

"Kayleigh! Hey Kayleigh! Over here!" Andy's voice rose above the excited shouts of children and adults. He was standing in line near the Tilt-A-Whirl, waving me over. I jogged over to him.

"This is one of my favorites!" he said, his voice raised in excitement. "Wanna go with me?"

I like the Tilt-A-Whirl, too . . . but my favorite ride is the Salt and Pepper Shaker. That's a cool ride, but Andy doesn't like it. Every time he rides it, he says he feels like he's going to barf.

27

"Not now," I said. "I want to check something out." I craned my neck in the direction of the tents at the other end of the carnival. "I want to go check out that clown tent."

Andy frowned and wrinkled his nose. "Why do you want to go there *now?*" he asked.

"I just want to go check it out. Are you coming?"

Andy shook his head. "You're on your own," he replied. "I'm going for a ride."

I turned and looked at the red and white striped tents in the distance.

And I started walking.

Carnivals are lots of fun. As I walked along the midway, I saw kids playing games and winning stuffed animals. Well, some were winning stuffed animals, anyway. I never had much luck at games. Once I won a four-foot stuffed lion, but that's about it.

But once again, the clown's words began running through my head, repeating over and over. I tried to stop thinking about him, but I couldn't. I just knew that something was not right. What it was, I didn't know. Maybe if I investigated the clown tent, I'd figure it out.

Clowns are supposed to be funny, aren't they? *Aren't they?*

How come these clowns just didn't seem that funny—or friendly?

Enjoy the rides, the clown sneered in my head. I shook his voice away, but it came back again. *Enjoy the rides . . . .*

As I approached the clown tent, I slowed down. I decided that it would probably be best if I stayed out of sight.

I walked a bit farther and saw the sign on the tent:

KLOWNS ONLY - ALL OTHERS KEEP OUT

Not a very friendly sign.

I slipped alongside the tent, turning my head quickly to make sure no one was watching. A few feet from the opening of the tent was a big, canvas tarp piled up, and I was able to crawl beneath it and be completely hidden. Here I could peer out and watch the clowns as they came and left the tent. I wanted to get a better look at more of them, to see if they all had that same, sinister glare.

I didn't have to wait long.

A clown seemed to come from out of nowhere, striding down the midway in big, oversized shoes.

He was holding a bouquet of balloons in his hand, and he walked right up to the entrance of the tent — and stopped.

Slowly, the clown looked to the left and to the right. It looked like he was checking to make sure that no one was watching him.

Then I had a horrible thought. What if he knew he was being watched? What if he found me?

From my hiding place I crossed my fingers, hoping for the best.

The clown kept turning his head, looking, looking — then he stopped. Apparently satisfied, he strode into the tent.

There were other clowns in the tent, too. I could hear them talking now, chuckling to themselves. But there was something strange about that, too.

Suddenly, I realized what it was! Their voices! *They all sounded the same!* They all had that same, deep, gruff growl that the clown at the ticket booth had.

Spooky.

From my hiding place, I listened intently. It sounded like some of them were eating. Maybe they were on lunch break.

All at once, all of the clowns stopped talking,

except for one. His voice was louder than the others. He spoke with a nasty snarl, and his voice filled the tent. He was angry.

And from where I was hiding only a few feet away, I heard every chilling word that he said.

"There's just too many of them around here," the clown snarled angrily. *"They're enjoying themselves now, but I say we get rid of them. Let's get rid of all of them. I want them dead. All of them!"*

I gasped, and covered my mouth with my hand. *Oh my gosh!* I thought. See? I knew that these clowns were up to something! They were plotting something horrible!

I was terrified. I was hidden, but what if they found me? What then?

I burrowed farther beneath the tarp and curled up into a ball.

Wait a minute, I thought. *I can't stay here forever. I have to go warn someone. I have to call the police! Yes, that's it! I'll go call 9-1-1!*

But I'll have to make sure the clowns don't catch me.

I pulled a portion of the tarp back, just enough so I could see a tiny bit.

There.

Right in front of me, just a few inches away, was the bottom of the tent. If I was really, really, extra, extra careful, I could reach out and pull the side of the tent up just a tiny bit — not even an inch — and look inside the tent. Then, when all of the clowns were gone, I could run from my hiding place and call the police.

I slowly reached forward and fumbled with the bottom of the tent. The heavy white canvas felt like old denim beneath my fingers.

I pulled it up just a teensy, tiny bit — and there they were.

The clowns were seated around a picnic table. I was right! They were on lunch break.

Just then, another clown came into view. He had been on the other side of the tent, and I hadn't seen him. He had something in his hand, but I couldn't see what it was.

But I could tell by the tone of his voice that he meant business. He sounded angry and mean.

"This'll teach 'em," he growled. "I'm gonna kill 'em all."

Suddenly there was a popping sound, and then the sound of —

Spraying?

That's what it was. As I watched, I could see the clown bending over a bench, spraying something. "This'll get rid of 'em," he said, sweeping back and forth with a can of —

Ant killer! That's what he had been talking about! He was only killing ants that were climbing around on the picnic table!

Suddenly I felt very foolish. Very, very, foolish. I was glad I hadn't gone to call the police, after all. I sure would've looked silly. And I probably would've got into some big trouble as well.

I relaxed a bit, and began to think the whole thing was actually pretty funny. My imagination often runs wild, and this time it had sure taken me for a ride. I actually had to try hard to keep from giggling in my hiding place.

But it still didn't change the way I felt about the clowns. As I looked at them, it was easy to see that they all had that same, eerie smile. In fact, they never *stopped* smiling. They smiled all the time.

That's crazy. No one smiles *all* the time, no

35

matter how happy they are. Something weird was definitely going on here, that was for sure.

One by one, the clowns got up and left the tent. They walked right past me, only a few feet away. I'm sure they had no idea that a twelve year-old girl was hiding beneath the tarp right next to their tent.

I was getting kind of antsy to go on the rides. I had been hiding for almost a half an hour, and I was getting bored.

And *hot*. The sun had been baking the canvas I was hiding under, and it was like being in an oven. A bead of sweat trickled down my forehead and dribbled down my nose. If I stayed here much longer, I'd be well-done!

After what seemed like hours, the last clown got up from the picnic table. He tossed a paper plate and an empty cup into the waste basket and left, walking right past me.

Finally. I would wait just another minute or so, then leave.

But as fate would have it, a minute wouldn't have the chance to go by. Because right then, at that very moment, the tarp suddenly exploded up and away from me! Bright sunlight shone down, and I squinted.

It was hard to see in the intense light, but there

was no mistaking what the dark shadow looming above me was.

A clown.

Not just a clown, but *the* clown. The same clown that had sold me my tickets. The same clown that had grabbed my arm.

That same, wicked grin.

That same green hair.

The same leering, piercing eyes.

He was standing over me, holding the tarp in his hand—and he didn't look happy. He didn't look happy at all.

7

My mind raced a zillion miles an hour. What could I do? Run? No, he was too close to me. He'd catch me for sure.

I was trapped. There was nothing I could do, nowhere I could go. Even if I screamed my head off, the noise from the carnival and the whirring rides would drown out my cries for help.

Suddenly, the clown moved his arm. Very slowly, he reached out his hand to me. Not for me to take, but to extend a gesture.

His hand turned palm-up, and he curled one finger toward him, indicating for me to come with him, or stand up, or something. Behind his hand, his face was a frozen mask, with a phony, fake smile.

His finger continued to curl, beckoning, urging me on.

Right! I'm not going anywhere with some kooky, crazy-looking clown!

Then he slowly leaned over, blocking out the sun completely. I could see his features clearly: his bulbous, red nose, his white, pasty make-up, his glaring eyes, his mad, catlike grin.

All around me, the sights and sounds of the carnival filled the air. Again, I thought about screaming, but it would be impossible for anyone to hear me. And there was no one around to see what was going on.

I was a goner.

The clown's mouth moved. He spoke in that same, gruff hiss.

"No clowning around," he said. His voice was rough and raspy. "No clowning around, Kayleigh."

Oh my gosh! He knew my name! How did he know who I was?!?!

I freaked. There wasn't anything to do but run, and I knew it. It was the only chance I had.

In a sudden explosive movement I sprang to my feet and bolted, taking one giant leap and then running like I had never ran before. My sneakers pounded the thick green grass, and I stretched my legs as far as I could in an effort to push myself even faster. I sprinted toward the midway, not looking back, certain that the clown was right on my heels.

Everything around me was a blur of colors and flashing lights and loud music and people. I hardly noticed what was going on around me. The only thing I concentrated on was getting away from the clown.

How did he know my name? I thought. That was probably the scariest part.

If I can only make it to the midway, I thought. *I'll be safe there. If I can only make it to the midway . . . .*

I passed a spinning merry-go-round, filled with candy-stripe poles and multicolored, shiny horses. A popcorn trailer whizzed by on my left, followed by a kiddie roller coaster.

And I didn't look back. I couldn't.

Run faster! I urged myself. *Faster! Faster!*

As I reached the carnival midway, my fear began to drain away. With all of these people around, I was sure that someone would help if the clown was after me.

I slowed to a jog, my lungs heaving and my heart pounding. My jog turned into a fast gate, then a steady, brisk walk.

I stopped, my breath still heaving in and out. I turned to look back.

The clown was gone! There was no sign of him anywhere!

I snapped my head around, searching the crowd around me for any sign of him. My pulse quickened, my heart throbbed, and I held my breath as my eyes scanned the mob of people around me.

Where had he gone? Was he after me? It would be easy to miss him in the crowd of people.

Satisfied that he was nowhere near, I bent over to catch my breath. I placed my hands on my legs just above my knees, staring at the ground. I could hear my heart throbbing, bouncing in my chest like a trampoline.

But I had escaped. I was all right, and I began to breathe easier.

Find Andy, I thought. *Find Andy and tell him that something's going on. Something with the clowns.*

I relaxed, stood up, turned . . . and gasped in horror.

I was face to face — with a clown.

This time, I *did* scream. The clown's face was only inches from mine, and the sudden shock made me shriek out loud.

"Good grief!" the clown said . . . but his lips never moved! His arm came up and grabbed his chin . . . *and pulled it up over his head!*

It was Andy!

"Like . . . what's up with you?" he asked, scrunching his forehead and squinting.

"You scared me, that's what's up with me!" I

answered, my voice rising above the noise around us.

"Isn't it cool?" Andy said, lifting the clown mask into the air to show me. "I won it over at the softball toss. I got two out of three! That's how I got this cool mask!"

He put it back over his face, and I grimaced. The clown face wasn't scary, but I had seen just about enough clowns for one day.

"Andy," I said, my eyes searching the crowd around us. "There's something really wrong with the clowns. I mean . . . they're nuts or something. I'm sure of it."

Andy crinkled his nose. "They're clowns," he said. "They're supposed to be a little nuts."

I told him what had happened to me over at the tent. "He knew my name!" I said. "He knew my name! How did he know my name?!?!?"

Andy got this really funny look on his face. "Maybe it's because it's printed on your shirt," he said, his voice reeking with mockery.

I glanced down at my shirt, but I knew instantly that Andy was right. This was my T-shirt from band camp. It has our school logo on the back, and my name embroidered on the front.

Whoops. I guess it wasn't really a mystery how the clown knew my name, after all. Boy, did I feel foolish!

Even so, I knew that something about the clowns just wasn't right. I *knew* it.

"Come on," I urged Andy. "I want to go back to that tent and find out what is really going on around here."

Andy shook his head. He clearly wasn't interested, but I was persistent. "Just for a few minutes," I pressed. "Let's look around the clown tent. We don't have to go inside. I just want to see if there's anything strange around there."

"Like . . . besides *you?*" Andy sneered.

"I'm serious!" I pleaded. "It'll only take five minutes!"

Andy continued to shake his head. "Not me," he said. "I want to go and ride some more rides and play some more games. I don't care about any dumb clowns."

I dug into my pocket and pulled out a small roll of yellow stubs. I handed them to him.

"Here," I said. "Here's five tickets for five rides. You can have them . . . but only if you go with me."

Andy tried to grab them but I pulled them out of reach. His hand grasped empty air.

"Only if you go with me," I repeated, frowning.

45

I held the tickets in the air, dangling them like a worm on a hook.

He took the bait.

"Deal," he said. His arm shot out again, and I made no effort to pull the tickets away this time. He snatched them out of my hand and stuffed them into his pocket. "Let's go get this over with."

We approached the tent with caution, looking around to make sure there weren't any clowns in sight. So far, the only ones we had seen were the ones that were in charge of running the rides. A few of them looked at us, but I looked away. They gave me the creeps.

We walked around to the back of the tent, but we couldn't get all the way around it since it had been set up so close to the fence. We turned around and walked in the opposite direction, walking in front of the tent, past the entryway.

"There," I whispered as we passed by the place I had been hiding not ten minutes ago. *"That's where I was hiding. That's where that clown found me. I was hidden pretty good. At least, I thought I was. I don't know how he found —"*

Andy's firm grasp on my wrist silenced the rest of my sentence. We stopped walking.

Andy was staring at something behind one of

the rides. I followed his gaze, trying to figure out what he was looking at. All I could see was a tangled web of steel pipes and braces that held the ride together.

Until something moved.

"Right there," he said. In the dark shadows behind the Ferris wheel, I saw something.

A clown.

"Is that him?" Andy asked.

He was standing in the shadows, and I couldn't see him real well . . . but I could see him well enough. Well enough to know.

It was the same clown that had found me under the tarp! The same clown that had sold me my tickets!

"Yes!" I answered excitedly. "That's him! I'd know him anywhere!"

The clown was acting strange. He was looking around, making sure that no one else was watching him. He was acting very suspicious.

Andy and I didn't move a muscle. We were standing in front of the tent, in full view. If we flinched, we'd be seen for sure. If we stayed frozen, maybe the clown wouldn't see us.

Maybe.

What happened next is hard to explain . . . but

the clown *vanished!* One moment he was there—the next, he was gone!

"Where did he go?!?!" Andy asked. "He was there just a second ago!"

"I don't know," I answered, "but he sure is acting kooky. I *told* you something is weird about these clowns!"

Andy started walking toward the place where the clown had just been.

Not me! I stayed right where I was. I'd seen enough clowns. Especially *that* clown.

"What are you doing?!?!" I called out. Andy turned his head while he walked. "I'm going to see where he went," he replied. "Are you coming?"

Why I said 'yes', I'll never know.

We walked behind and beneath the enormous ride. Above and around us, gears cranked and metal churned. The roar was deafening. Kids screamed in delight as the huge ride swooped them through the air.

We ducked under and around beams. Andy led the way, and I followed.

But I spotted the door first.

"Look," I said, leaning toward Andy shouting into his ear. *"Right there."*

It was a door, all right. It was tucked in the

shadows behind a tangled mass of pipes. Actually, I'm surprised that I even saw it. It was really hidden.

"I'll bet that's where he went," Andy said. He took a step toward the door, reached for the large, metal doorknob, and turned to face me.

"Wanna go find out where he went?" he asked. A smirk was on his face, and I knew that there was no stopping him. I knew that even if I said 'no', he'd still go.

Alone.

What could I do? He's my brother. I couldn't let him go alone.

Besides . . . I guess, if the truth must be known, I really was curious. I wanted to know why the clown was acting the way he was.

And I wanted to know where he went.

So when Andy turned the knob and pulled the door open, I followed. I didn't even think twice about it.

Unfortunately, *opening* that door was a big mistake.

Deciding to go *through* the door was even worse.

And we were about to find out in a horrible, horrible way.

49

Darkness.

As soon as we stepped through the door, we were in total darkness. Andy and I stood for a moment, allowing our eyes to adjust to the murky gloom. I could tell that we were in some sort of hallway, but that was about it. I couldn't see anything more.

The sounds of the carnival were muffled, too. It was as if we had taken one giant step far away. We could still hear the grinding of the Ferris wheel and the lively shouts of people enjoying the rides and games, but now the sounds were muddier and not nearly as loud as they had been.

"*Come on,*" Andy whispered. He took a step forward, and I followed. We walked for a few feet, then stopped. The hall turned to the left, and the floor seemed to slant downward.

And it was *dark*. There was no light at all.

Still, we walked. As soon as Andy turned, he simply disappeared. I mean . . . it was *dark!* But I found that if I held my arms out, I could brush my fingers along the wall. I felt safer doing that, I guess.

We walked for a few seconds, and then I could see a dim light forming in front of us. Ahead, the hall seemed to open up. A faint, red glow—very, very faint—could be seen.

And something else.

The clown.

He was right in front of us, no more than ten feet.

Andy stopped, and I bumped into him. Thankfully, we didn't make any noise.

The clown was standing in one spot, looking the other way. I could barely see him. He was just a shadowy figure in a dim red light.

Suddenly, he turned and was gone! He turned

to the right, and vanished into another room. Where he was going, I hadn't a clue.

But now I *wanted* to know. I *had* to know.

I stepped around Andy and slowly made my way to where the clown had been standing. Andy followed behind me.

The hall ended, and in the red glow I could make out that we were in a big room. It was still very dark, and all I could see were shadows.

Until I turned.

I was going to say something to Andy, but what it was, I don't even remember.

The only thing I knew for sure was that the figure now looming over us was definitely *not* a clown.

It was a vampire.

How did I know it was a vampire? Easy. Even though it was dark, he was so close to me that I could make out every little detail about him.

He was dressed in a tight-fitting black suit, and had a white shirt with ruffles down the front. A shiny black cape was draped over his shoulders. His hair was black and slicked back, and his skin was a real weird, creamy color. His mouth was open, showing two long fangs on both sides of his mouth. He was horrifying.

If you've never felt blood drain completely from your face, let me tell you about it — because when I saw the dark shape of the vampire, that's exactly what happened. The feeling starts at the top of your head and works its way down around your ears, then back around to your face. It's a dizzying, light-headed feeling, and as the blood left my face I could feel my skin tingling. Soon, my whole head felt cold and strange.

Okay, maybe *all* of the blood didn't drain from my face, but that's sure what it felt like.

As for Andy — he passed out! And I mean he *passed out!* He fainted right then and there. If I hadn't reached out to catch him before he stumbled, he would have fell smack dab on his face.

But the vampire never moved. He stayed frozen in place, staring at me, one arm raised, reaching outward. Andy was limp in my arms but he was coming back around, so I gently lowered him to the floor.

When I looked up again, I felt foolish for the *second* time that day.

The 'vampire' was nothing but a wax dummy! He was staring past me into space, motionless. When I stood straight up, it looked like he was staring directly at me.

Don't laugh . . . if you were me, you would've freaked out, too.

Then I figured it out!

We must be in the Haunted House! I had spotted the sign on the front earlier, but I didn't give it much thought. We must've come in through the back door! Usually, I stay away from the Haunted House. I'd rather spend my tickets on a ride or a game.

Andy came to, and he slowly got to his feet.

"Wh . . . what ha . . . ha . . . happened?" he stammered, rubbing his forehead with the palm of his hand.

"I saved you from the evil Count Wax-ula," I said, pointing at the gruesome form of the vampire. Andy turned, saw the figure, and jumped. Hah! Got him twice with the same thing.

"Don't worry," I explained. "He's only a wax dummy."

Andy stared at the tall figure for a moment, shaking his head from side to side. "Man, he sure looks real," he said.

"Come on," I urged. "Let's get out of here."

"But we don't know where the clown went," Andy protested.

"I don't care. This place creeps me out.

57

Besides . . . I'm sure we're not supposed to be here."

We made our way back the way we came in, through the pitch-black hallway. In the darkness, I fumbled with my hands and, thankfully, found the door.

My thankfulness turned to all-out terror in the blink of an eye—because when I tried to turn the door handle, it wouldn't budge! I pulled and pushed, trying to get it open.

But it was no use. The door knob didn't move an inch. The door was locked.

We were trapped.

Trapped—in the Haunted House.

Some birthday this was turning out to be.

The doorknob was frozen solid in my hands.
I tried turning it both ways, but it wouldn't budge.

"It's . . . It's locked!" I said to Andy. He
brushed past me in the darkness, and I could hear him
pulling at the doorknob, trying to force the door open.

But it was no use. The door was locked tight.

"There has to be a way out of here," he said.
"Come on. Let's go find the front door."

Once again, we walked through the dark

hallway and past the wax vampire, only this time, we made our way across the room to another hallway — and I knew for sure we were in the Haunted House.

A single, tiny red bulb glowed from the ceiling, giving off just enough light to see. I gasped, more from wonder and surprise than from fear.

The hall was lined with a dozen wax figures. And there were some weird things, too. The first one, to my left, was a werewolf. He had dark hair all over his body. Like the vampire, his mouth was open, exposing two rows of sharp teeth. His arms were raised, showing strong-looking, sharp claws.

On the right, next to Andy, was a mummy. It was wrapped tightly in white cloth, and its arms were upraised, straight out, just like you'd expect a mummy to look like.

"This place is cool!" Andy whispered excitedly, walking slowly down the hall. I followed.

There were more wax figures. A shiny, silver space alien held out a ray gun, ready for action. A swashbuckling pirate held a sword up, fighting some imaginary opponent. He had a thick black mustache and beard, and he wore a black hat with the familiar skull and crossbones logo on it.

There was also a crazy-looking swamp

creature. He was hunched down like he was coming up out of the water. Seaweed covered his shoulders and his head, hiding most of his gruesome, slimy face. I think if I saw that coming toward me in a lake, I'd never go swimming again.

All in all, there were exactly thirteen wax figures. They sure did look real. Someone had spent a lot of time and talent to make them look the way they did.

But it was the last figure on the left that made me freeze in shock. I knew it was only wax, but it was far, far, too creepy. And too real looking.

It was a clown. He looked just like all of the other clowns we'd seen, only this one looked, well — *different*. There was something about this clown that was different from the ones that were working at the carnival.

After I got over my initial shock, I relaxed. *Sheesh, Kayleigh,* I thought. *Get over it. It's a wax clown. Get a grip, wouldja?*

Meanwhile, Andy had followed yet another hall that went off to the right. I took one more glance at all of the wax figures that lined the hall, and looked down the hall at Andy. I could see him kneeling down, staring at something.

"Hey Kayleigh!" he said. "Come check this

61

out!"

I had just started off toward him when a hand came out of nowhere and tightly clasped my shoulder.

The hand jerked me back around, and I screamed.

The clown! He wasn't wax after all! He was real! He was real—and he had a tight grip on my shoulder. I couldn't get away if I tried!

"I thought I heard someone in here," he said angrily. "Didn't you read the sign?!?!?"

My scream had brought Andy running, and he stopped next to me.

"Didn't you read the sign?!?!?" the clown asked again.

63

I was too afraid to speak. Then I felt his grip soften, and he let me go. I didn't waste any time taking a step back.

"What sign?" Andy asked.

"The sign on the front of the Haunted House," the clown snapped. "It clearly says that the Haunted House isn't open yet. You shouldn't be in here."

"We're sorry," I managed to say. "We were just curious." I didn't tell him that we'd followed a clown in through the back door.

"I'll escort you out the door. You must leave immediately. Come."

The clown turned and began walking. Andy and I followed. We turned down long halls and went through dark rooms. The place was spooky.

Just like a Haunted House should be.

Soon, we came to a room that was brightly lit. I could see the clown clearly now, and what a sight he was!

He wore a one piece, oversized white body suit with red polka-dots all over it. His hair was blue and curly. He had a round, red, plastic ball over his nose. White powder covered his face, and red lipstick painted a continual smile from ear to ear. In the light, he didn't look near as threatening as he had in the gloom of the hallway. In fact, he looked downright

64

comical.

He strode across the room to a door, and opened it. Outside, the carnival came into view, and the sounds suddenly filled the room. The clown stood patiently, holding the door open, waiting for us.

Andy took the lead, and I followed. At the door, I stopped.

"Who . . . who *are* you?" I asked.

"I am Klaus Von Klown," he replied, still holding the door. With one hand, he reached up and plucked off his nose. Then he reached up and pulled his wig off! Now he looked more — well, more *human*. A human with an awful lot of make-up.

"I am Klaus Von Klown," he repeated, "and this is my carnival. Do you like it?"

Andy was just outside the door, waiting for me. "You bet!" he answered. I just nodded my head. I began to think that maybe I was the nutty one. There wasn't anything wrong with the clowns at all. They were just hard-working people, doing their jobs, making people laugh. I felt silly.

Until Klaus Von Klown spoke again. I had just stepped through the door, and I could hear it begin to squeak shut behind me. Klaus Von Klown's voice stopped me cold and sent shivers from the top of my head to the tip of my toes.

"Enjoy the rides," he said, laughing. *"Enjoy the rides . . . ."*

It was horrible. Klaus Von Klown's voice was exactly the same as the other clown voices! And I mean *exactly*. They were identical.

How could that be?

Andy had already started off toward the midway, and I ran up to him.

"Klaus Von Klown's voice sounds just like the other clowns!" I said. "It's exactly the same!"

Andy looked at me like I was from outer space. "Big deal," he replied. "Lots of people sound alike. So what?"

"Not just *alike*," I answered, shaking my head. *"Exactly.* They all sound perfectly identical. Klaus Von Klown said 'enjoy the rides' . . . and it sounded just like the clown that took our tickets! It was his voice, *exactly!"*

"You've got a pretty wild imagination," Andy said. "You should write books or something . . . like that kooky guy up north that writes the series of scary books." And with that, he turned and began walking toward one of the rides.

Fine. He can go and do whatever he wants. He can go on the rides, play the games, whatever.

Not me. I was going to find out what was going on. And the first place I was going to look was at the clown tent.

I strode along the midway, watching everyone. Sometimes it can be entertaining to go places and just watch people. It can be a lot of fun, watching *them* have fun.

Near the Tilt-A-Whirl, I saw a little boy holding a balloon in one hand and a huge ice cream cone in the other. His lips, his nose and his cheeks were plastered with gooey brown and white ice cream. Every time he took a bite from the cone, he smeared more ice-cream onto his face. He looked funny and cute.

Then I saw a man playing the rubber ducky game. That's a game where water swirls around in a small wading pool. You get to pick one duck, and win the prize that is written on the bottom of the duck. Most of the prizes are just small, cheap toys. But if you pick the right duck, you win a BIG prize — a huge, stuffed teddy bear.

Well, when the man leaned over to pick out a duck, a woman behind him wasn't paying attention. She was talking to another woman, and they both started laughing like hyenas. One of the women backed up and bumped into the man . . . sending him head over heels right into the pool! It was hilarious. Every inch of his body was soaked.

People-watching really *can* be a lot of fun.

But every so often, I caught a glimpse of a clown. They seemed to be everywhere . . . working in booths, behind counters, and taking tickets for the rides.

By now, I knew something was up. I *knew* that something wasn't right about these clowns. There was no doubt about it. I felt like running right up to one of them and asking something like *'hey . . . what's the matter with you guys, anyway?'*

But I didn't. Deep down, I was afraid of them.

Deep down, I thought that if *they* knew that *I* knew, I'd be in trouble.

Big trouble.

I continued walking and made my way directly to the clown tent. I turned and looked around to make sure that no one was watching, then I turned back around and peered into the tent.

No clowns. No one was in sight.

I turned back around again, checking to make sure that no one was nearby, then I turned back — and slipped quickly into the tent.

And what I was about to find was worse than anything I could have possibly imagined.

First, I walked over to the picnic table covered by a red and white checkered tablecloth. Sitting on the tablecloth was a pitcher of thick, pea-colored juice, and a few clear plastic cups. Some of the cups were empty, but some of the cups still had a little bit of juice left in them. It didn't look like any kind of juice I'd seen before.

I picked up one of the half-filled cups and held it under my nose.

It smelled horrible! Ugh! It was *nasty!* It had

a strong, chemical smell that burned my nostrils. For a moment, I thought I was going to puke.

I recoiled and dropped the cup. The green juice spilled all over the grass at my feet. I leapt back and pinched my nose closed with my fingers. Ick. The awful smell lingered on for a moment, and I waved my hand back and forth in front of my face. I wasn't going to smell that stuff again!

But I was curious. What on earth was in that juice? Nobody could drink that stuff!

I looked at the ground where the cup had spilled.

Oh my gosh!

The grass that had come in contact with the juice was dead! It had turned from a dark, forest green to a brittle, dry brown! The juice killed the grass!

Whatever the green liquid was, it sure wasn't fruit juice.

Wow! Was I glad I didn't take a sip!

But then I thought about it. Were the clowns drinking this stuff? If they were, they'd have to have some pretty tough stomachs.

Than again, no. There's no way anyone could drink that stuff. It's poison. Surely, if someone drank it, they'd be dead in five seconds.

Then a wave of horror rushed through me like water, seeping through my skin and into my bones.

What was their plan? What were these clowns using the 'juice' for?

I had an answer, but I couldn't bear to even *think* it.

On the other side of the tent was a row of flaps. Behind each flap was a small, private room. Perhaps this was where the clowns put on their make up. I didn't see any movement, and it didn't look like any of the clowns were inside of the rooms.

I hoped.

I stepped around the acid stain and walked cautiously over to the row of flaps, tip-toeing silently through the soft grass.

I stopped, listening for any signs of movement. I heard nothing, except for the continuous music and laughter and bells from the bustling carnival.

I stepped over to one of the closed flaps, slowly reaching my hand out.

Should I do it? Should I find out what's behind the flap?

I turned my head, making sure that none of the clowns had returned. There was no one there. I was the only one in the tent.

Slowly, carefully, I grasped the canvas flap and

73

pulled it back. I peered inside, and let out a sigh of relief.

No clown. Whew.

Behind the flap was a small room. The walls were canvas, and there was a small wood desk with a single metal folding chair in front of it. On the desk was an array of clown make-up: lipstick, powder, paint. Two wigs—one with green hair, one with orange hair—sat on the edge of the desk. A pair of big, red, floppy shoes sat in the grass next to the chair.

It was just as I had suspected. These 'rooms' were used by the clowns to put their make-up on.

I should have left it at that. There wasn't anything more to see, and I should have just left.

But I didn't. I wanted to see if there was anything else in any of the other rooms. So I closed the flap from the first room, and took a step toward the next one.

I reached my hand out, grasped the flap, and stopped. I suddenly had a very strange feeling. It was like a warning, telling me not to go any farther, to let go of the flap. The feeling was really weird. I almost turned and ran.

But no. I ignored the strange sensation, and drew the canvas flap aside.

I immediately wished I hadn't.

I gasped. I froze. Horror hit me like an invisible freight train. Every single hair on my body was electrified, standing on end. I was covered in goose bumps from head to toe.

Because in the tiny room, lying on the grass on his stomach, was a clown.

A clown—with no head.

It was a horror so shocking, so powerful that I felt faint. I started to shake.

The clown's arms were spread wide, bird-like. He was wearing a baggy yellow shirt with blue stripes. Wide, rainbow-colored suspenders supported oversize, black and white checkered pants.

But by far the most gruesome sight was the fact that he clearly had no head.

Except—

There was something odd going on. The clown

was decapitated . . . his head was definitely missing, yet there was no blood around anywhere. There was no sign of any fight or struggle.

And when I leaned closer, I had my answer.

There were wires and metal pieces coming out of the clown's neck!

He was a *robot!*

My fear faded, turning to amazement and wonder.

Robots?!?!? Robot *clowns?!?!?*

I stepped into the small room and let go of the canvas door flap. I was alone in the tiny space — alone with a broken robot clown.

Andy was going to be sorry he didn't come with me!

I knelt closer to the clown to get a better look. My knees sank into the soft grass.

He was a robot, all right. Colorful wires protruded out from his neck. There appeared to be circuit boards and other small panels. My dad had to fix his computer one day, and he had to take the cover off. Inside were wires and buttons and things.

That's what the clown's neck looked like! A bundle of computer stuff.

My mind spun like a furious top.

Were they all robots? Could all of the clowns be

78

robots?

It was like a weird science fiction movie that came to life.

Robot clowns. I didn't even like the *sound* of it.

Then I wondered something else: where did the clown's head go? Maybe it was out for repair. Maybe the clown's head was being examined. The idea sounded funny, and I almost laughed out loud.

Almost.

And it was a good thing I didn't. Because right at that exact moment, I heard a voice. A voice that I recognized instantly. It was gruff and low, and sounded mean. I froze.

"It's almost time," I heard the clown say. "It's almost time."

A clown had come into the tent! For the second time today, I was trapped.

My heart jumped up and down like a pogo stick bouncing around inside of me. Instantly, I spun and peeked beneath the door flap. There was a tiny crack I could peer through, and I strained my eyes to get a glimpse.

The clown was standing by the picnic table—drinking the weird green juice! Ugh! I almost puked just looking at him! How could he drink the stuff?!?!?

Duh, Kayleigh, I thought. *If he's a robot, it probably won't hurt him. The green juice is probably what powers them.*

The clown placed the cup back on the picnic table, turned, and began walking —

Toward me!

Oh no! He was walking directly toward me!

I stood up quickly and quietly, and backed against the side of the canvas. If I thought my heart was jumping like a pogo stick before, it was nothing compared to what it was doing now. My heart pounded like a basketball on a gym court.

I could hear the clown's feet pad the thick grass.

Closer . . . .

What could I do?

Closer . . . .

I couldn't run. There was no place to hide.

Closer . . . .

I stood there, frantically trying to come up with a plan for escape, when the canvas flap I was hiding behind was suddenly thrust open!

How do I get myself into these situations? I would have given anything to be somewhere else at that moment. Anywhere else, I didn't care. I just didn't want to be *there*.

The canvas flap was suddenly in my face. I could see the clown's arm just inches away.

Did he see me? I was backed up against the canvas wall, next to the door . . . but when the clown opened the flap, he swung it back . . . covering me up! He couldn't see me!

Apparently satisfied with whatever he saw, his arm vanished and the flap fell down, closed.

I felt like I had just won the Grand Prize at the rubber ducky game.

That had been a close one.

There was more commotion coming from inside the tent, and I crouched down again to look through the crack in the bottom of the tent flap.

Another clown! And another! Now there were three clowns in the tent! They were standing close to one another, talking. But their voices were so low that I couldn't hear what they were saying.

Smart, Kayleigh, really smart, I thought. *A fine mess you're in now, birthday girl.*

I wished Andy was with me. Sure, he can be a goof sometimes, but he's got a knack for getting out of jams.

And this was a jam. A *big* jam.

But what were the clowns up to? What was going on?

One of the clowns picked up the pitcher of green juice and poured three glasses. They drank them down, then placed the cups back on the table.

Suddenly they left, just as quickly as they had arrived. They turned and walked out of the tent.

It was the chance I needed. I wanted to get out

of there, to go find Andy and tell him what I had seen. He wouldn't believe me, of course, and would want to see for himself. I wouldn't blame him. If someone told me that they'd seen a robot clown with no head, I'd want to see for myself, too.

Double-checking to make sure that no clowns were around, I slowly drew back the flap.

Cautiously . . . carefully . . . .

Nobody here. The tent was empty. Whew!

I heaved a heavy sigh of relief, and slipped from the room into the tent. I wanted to run. I wanted to fly through the tent and never look back, forgetting about clowns and robots and smelly green juice.

But no. Andy wouldn't believe me. He'd never believe a word of what I told him.

So I decided that I would *show* him.

I walked quickly to the picnic table, and picked up the pitcher. I glanced up at the tent opening to make sure that no one was looking or coming.

Then I quickly poured the green liquid into a plastic cup until it was half full. I set the pitcher back down on the table and, holding the cup far from my nose, walked out of the tent.

Or, I *tried* to walk out of the tent. But I couldn't.

Because the big, dark form of Klaus Von Klown stood right in the doorway, glaring at me — blocking the way.

17

"Going somewhere?" Klaus Von Klown asked. His eyes flickered from my face to the cup, and back to my face.

I had to think fast.

"I, uh . . . ummm . . . ." I stammered. *Come on Kayleigh,* I thought. *Think of something! Think of something now!*

"Yes?" Klaus Von Klown urged. "You were saying?"

"I just, ummmm . . . was thirsty. Yes, I was

thirsty. I saw the juice, and it looked good." I raised the glass up near my lips and held my breath, not wanting to smell the putrid odor of the green goo.

All of a sudden Klaus Von Klown grabbed the cup from my hand! He did it so fast that I didn't even have time to pull away.

"That is not for you to drink," he scolded.

He sure didn't have to tell *me* that!

"What are you doing here?" he asked. His eyes never left mine, and I could tell he meant business. The white make-up on his face had smeared, and his painted-on smile had faded. His wig was missing, and so was the red plastic bulb he'd had on his nose, but he still looked like a clown. He looked angry . . . but I didn't think he would hurt me.

At least . . . I hoped he wouldn't.

Klaus Von Klown looked around the tent. "So," he began, "just what kind of mischief have you been getting into, hmmm?" His gaze returned to me.

"Uh, nothing," I said. "I just, well, I guess I was curious. You know . . . I just wanted to see how the clowns put on their make-up and stuff."

"And what 'stuff' did you see?" he asked, his eyes burning into mine. He took a step closer, and I took a step back. I was not liking this one bit.

"Nothing," I quickly answered again, shaking

my head. "Nothing at all."

He took a another step closer. Again, I took a step back. Then, I had an idea.

Without even waiting for him to speak again, I turned and began to run . . . to the other side of the tent! I didn't look back, but I could tell I surprised him.

Good. Maybe that would give me just enough extra time to —

"*STOP!*" he shouted. "Stop now!"

He had to be kidding! There was *no way* I was stopping! I ran straight to the other side of the tent—and found the large tear in the canvas. I grabbed it with my hand and pulled. The canvas ripped, and as it did, I lifted my leg and pushed it through.

"*STOP!*" Klaus Von Klown shouted again. His voice was louder and closer, and I knew he was coming after me. But there was no way I was going to listen to him. I wanted out of that tent as soon as possible.

I stepped through the huge tear and pulled my other leg through. The fence was only inches away and I grabbed it, using it for support.

I was through! I made it.

Klaus Von Klown suddenly appeared at the

gaping hole, but he was a lot bigger than I was, and he couldn't slip through as easily as I could.

I didn't hang around. I ran as fast as I could between the fence and the tent. I could hear the shouts of Klaus Von Klown behind me, telling me to stop, to come back.

No way. I was leaving. I was going to find Andy, and we were leaving. Right now. There was no way I was staying a moment longer. Not at this carnival. Not with robot clowns running all over the place.

That was my next question. Where *was* Andy? He's got to be around here somewhere. But with so many people, it would be easy for him to become lost in the crowd.

My eyes darted frantically from ride to ride, trying to catch a glimpse of him. I scanned the games to see if he was playing any of them.

Nope.

I walked quickly by the concession stands. Suddenly, I saw a face I recognized . . . but it wasn't the face I wanted to see!

It was the clown. That same nasty-looking clown that had sold me my tickets. That same clown that had grabbed my wrist and held it like a vice. The same clown that spoke to me in that awful, wheezing rasp. When I saw him, his voice crept back into my mind.

Enjoy the rides. The words whirled in my brain. *Enjoy the rides, Kayleigh.*

Suddenly the clown turned and looked at me! He looked directly at me, and he knew I was looking at him.

From where he stood on the other side of the midway, I could see him glaring at me, leering at me with that gross smile. Lights glistened in his eyes, and his white face seemed to glow in the glare of the bright, neon lights.

And he had something in his hand. What was it? I was too far away to see exactly what it was.

As I watched, he blew up a long balloon. The balloon was long . . . longer than his arm. He tied the end off, then began twisting the balloon in knots, twirling it around.

It was a balloon animal! He had made a balloon animal, and he held it out, as if he wanted to give it to me. He nodded his head, as if to say *'it's okay, Kayleigh . . . come and get it. Come and get it, Kayleigh . . . .'*

I knew that's what he wanted me to do, but I wasn't going to budge. I shook my head from side to side.

A grim look came to his face. In one hand he held the balloon, in the other — a long hairpin. He touched the sharp tip of the hairpin to the balloon and it exploded. The animal vanished. I was too far away to hear the balloon pop over the roaring of the music and rides, but that was just as well.

I wanted out. I was leaving. But I had to find Andy! Where was he?

All of a sudden, two clowns came out of nowhere! They were walking quickly along the midway, but when they saw me, they started to run!

They were after me!

I fled. I turned and ran as fast as I could, around rides, past games and popcorn stands. Through swarms of people, past the ticket booth. I wanted out. I wanted out *now*.

I ran toward the fence, my feet pounding the hard-packed ground. But as I approached the entrance, I realized I had another problem.

A *bigger* problem.

The gate was closing! Two clowns were busy swinging the gates closed! There was no way I would be able to get there in time to get out!

In seconds, the gate had clanked into place. One of the clowns looped a heavy chain through the fence, pulled out a big steel padlock, and fastened the two chains together. They glared at me with sinister, terrible smiles.

I was trapped.

Not only was I trapped . . . but Andy — as well as hundreds of people — were trapped in the carnival.

Trapped in the carnival — with the clowns.

Hide.

It was the only thing I could think to do. I knew that the two clowns were chasing me, and it was only a matter of time before they found me.

I slipped into the crowd of people, hoping to blend in. If I could stay close to a large group, I think I would be hard to spot. There were a lot of other girls at the carnival, and I hoped to just mix in with everyone else.

Then . . . hope. I was looking across the

midway past the Merry-Go-Round—and spotted Andy! He was playing the softball toss game again.

He wouldn't be able to hear me if I shouted. Besides, if I did call out to him, I'd attract attention to myself. That wasn't something I wanted to do.

After carefully looking around to make sure no clowns were watching, I made a dash across the midway and slipped behind the Tilt-A-Whirl. Above me, the monstrous metal beast spun wildly, much to the delight of its excited riders. They whooped and hollered as they whirled, and colorful lights flashed like lightning.

I ducked behind a small concession trailer and then behind a few games. Andy was still at the softball toss, and by the look on his face, he wasn't having much luck this time.

I sprinted up to him, out of breath.

"Andy!" I panted. "We're locked in! Everyone here is trapped! We can't get out! We have to find a way out!"

Andy just stared at me. "Man, Kayleigh," he said, shaking his head and rolling his eyes. "You've got to lay off the cotton candy. All of that sugar is messing with your brain."

I explained everything I saw . . . the green juice, the headless clown, Klaus Von Klown in the tent.

Andy's expression changed from disdain to disbelief. I told him about the clown that had made the balloon animal, and about the two clowns that had been chasing me. And I told him about the clowns that had locked the gate.

"Why do they want to keep us here?" he asked.

"You got me," I said. "But I want out. We have to get out of here and tell somebody."

Andy looked around. "The fence is too high," he said. "We'd break our necks if we tried to climb out of here."

We stood for a moment, wondering what to do. Every few seconds, we caught a glimpse of a clown. Most of them were busy manning the rides or the games or the concessions, and they didn't pay any attention to us.

Robot clowns, I thought. *Were they all robots? Were they all robotic clowns?* It seemed impossible.

And why did they lock us in here? Why didn't they want anyone to leave? That was the scariest part of all.

Just what were they up to? What did they want?

"Let's go try the back entrance," Andy suggested. "There might be a way out. We might be able to slip through somewhere."

I knew it was a long shot, but we had to try. Maybe Andy was right. Maybe we could slip through the back gate, if it wasn't locked. Hopefully, there wouldn't be any clowns around.

We ducked behind the row of games and ran through the grass. Andy was still carrying the clown mask that he had won. I wished he would get rid of it. I didn't want to see anyone . . . or anything . . . that even looked a *little* bit like a clown!

We stopped running when we came to a row of tents. Behind us, the carnival surged on. Bright lights lit up the night sky like a neon city. Hundreds of people cheered and laughed, completely unaware of the clowns.

But I figured that everyone would know about the clowns soon enough. The clowns were up to something. Something awful, I was sure. It was just a matter of time.

"*Look!*" Andy whispered loudly. He raised his arm and pointed, crouching down into the shadow of a tent. I knelt down next to him in the grass, looking where he was pointing.

The back gate was open! Not very much, but it was open—and there wasn't a clown in sight.

"*Let's go!*" I whispered. I shot a quick glance over my shoulder to make sure no clowns were watching. We were still some distance from the gate, but I was sure that if we ran fast, we could be at the fence in a matter of seconds.

Andy bolted first and I followed. He ran madly behind the tent in the safety of its shadow.

We were going to make it—I thought.

But right when we reached the end of the tent and were about to begin our final sprint across the grass and to the gate, the unthinkable happened.

Clowns.

There were two of them, behind the tent. It was like they had been there all along, knowing that we were coming. They stepped directly into our path. We almost ran into them! In fact, Andy was running so fast that he wasn't able to stop. He didn't want to run into the clown, so he dove to the ground and rolled — right between the legs of one of the clowns!

If I hadn't been so terrified, I would've thought that it looked pretty funny.

Andy didn't waste any time leaping to his feet, still grasping his clown mask in one hand. I had already turned and began to run the other way, but the clowns had leapt into action themselves.

The chase was on.

We ran around tents, through dark shadows, under rides and behind trailers. I shot a glance back and saw the clowns in hot pursuit. We'd put some distance between them and us, but they were still on our heels.

And what was worse, when I turned back around, Andy was gone! A half second ago he was right in front of me. Now, he was nowhere to be seen!

"Kayleigh!" I suddenly heard him hiss. *"Over here! Quick!"*

He had sneaked below the metal beams of one of the rides. I couldn't see him at all.

Quickly, I ducked and crawled on my hands and knees through the darkness. Above me, the ride clanked and roared. It was deafening.

Then I could see Andy's dark shape. He was crouched down on the ground.

Now I knew where I was! The Haunted House! We were at the rear entrance of the Haunted House!

Andy had already opened the door and was

climbing through. I quickly followed, closing the door behind me. Had the clowns seen where we had gone? Did they spot us as we ducked beneath the ride?

I didn't want to take any chances. "Come on!" I exclaimed, and we hustled through the dark hall until we came to the hallway with the faint red light.

Behind us, we heard a noise.

A door opening, then closing. Footsteps.

Oh no! The clowns! They knew we were in the Haunted House!

"Quick!" I hissed. "We have to hide!"

We ran down the hall and came to the room with all of the wax figures.

Now what?

The thundering of footsteps behind us were growing louder. We were almost out of time. Soon, the clowns would be upon us.

"There's a coffin in the other room!" Andy hissed. "I saw it the last time we were here. It's empty! Go climb inside and close the lid!"

"*Say what?!?!*" I exclaimed. "Get into a coffin?!?!"

"It's our only chance! Hurry!"

"But what are *you* going to do?!?!" I asked. I could hear the footsteps growing louder still. The clowns were almost here.

"Never mind me," Andy replied. "I've got an idea. Hurry up! Get into the coffin and close the lid!"

I must admit, I sure didn't want to be climbing into any coffin! But there was no other option.

I sprang down the hall and into the dark room, leaving Andy alone with the wax figures. I hoped he knew what he was doing!

In the gloom, I could make out the dark shape of the coffin lying on the floor. It was open, and, thankfully, there didn't appear to be anyone inside.

Boy, was I glad about that!

I climbed inside the coffin, reached up, and closed the lid. It squeaked as it came down, and I gently lowered it over top of me.

I was in total, complete darkness — but at least I was hidden. It sure felt freaky, laying down inside a coffin.

Hopefully, the clowns wouldn't search here. I hoped that they wouldn't think to look for a girl in a coffin. Maybe, in the darkness, they wouldn't even see the large wooden box at all.

But what about Andy? What was he up to?

Slowly, quietly, I leaned over in the darkness and raised the lid of the coffin a tiny bit, just enough to see out the crack.

And the first thing I saw was a clown!

Wait a minute, I thought. *That's not a clown – that's Andy! That's Andy with his goofy clown mask!*

He had put the mask on and climbed into the row of wax dummies. There he stood, one hand at his forehead in a salute, the other draped over the shoulders of the werewolf! Andy looked like a wax figure!

It was a daring plan. Was it going to work? Would the clowns know that Andy wasn't a wax dummy at all? Would they find me in the coffin?

We were about to find out.

Two shadows.

The clowns came into view, walking slowly through the hall. I could see them moving cautiously, tip-toeing their way along. Their heads turned from side to side, searching.

Suddenly, one of them stopped . . . right in front of Andy! The second clown stopped as well, and both of them gazed around at the shadowy wax figures.

From my hiding place in the coffin, I

shuddered. *Don't move, Andy,* I thought. The clowns were right next to him. *Don't move. Don't even breathe . . . .*

One of the clowns took a step toward one of the wax figures. He was staring at the vampire, leaning close to get a better look. The other clown began walking . . . and came into the room where I was hiding.

Horror swirled inside of me, and I quietly closed the lid of the coffin. I was immersed in inky darkness.

I could hear the clown shuffling around the room, searching, his feet scraping the floor.

He was looking for us.

I bit my lower lip and closed my eyes. *Please don't find me, please don't find me,* I repeated in my mind, over and over. *Please don't find me, please don't find me . . . .*

The shuffling of feet stopped. The clown had to be standing right next to the coffin.

From the hall, I heard a muffled voice. I couldn't hear what was being said, but suddenly the clown that was next to the coffin began to walk away! I heard his footsteps going back into the hall.

It was risky, but I leaned up again and lifted the lid just a tiny, tiny bit.

Andy was still frozen in position, one hand held in a salute, the other draped across the shoulders of the snarling werewolf. It looked like he and the werewolf were buddies.

But it worked! The clowns must've decided that we weren't around, because they suddenly continued on down the hall! I could hear their footsteps fading away.

I wasn't in any hurry to move from my hiding place. At any moment the clowns might return, and then we'd be goners.

After what seemed like hours, I saw Andy move from his spot next to the werewolf. His head turned slowly, then he stepped away from the wax figures.

The coffin lid squeaked as I pushed it open, and I stood up. I stepped out and gently set the lid back down. Andy walked to my side.

"Whew," he whispered, his voice filled with relief. "That was close. Those clowns were right next to me."

"Good thing you didn't sneeze, huh?" I replied.

"Oh man," Andy said, removing the mask from his face. "Don't even think about that."

Except for the muffled sounds of the carnival outside, the Haunted House was quiet. Then, as we were trying to decide what to do, we heard a commotion down the hall! We heard frantic scuffling and the shuffling of feet. It surprised us and we jumped, ready to run back to our hiding places.

But the noise stopped, and we relaxed.

"Maybe the clowns left the Haunted House," I mused. "Maybe that's what the noise was."

We decided to take the chance. I was sure that the back door was locked, and Klaus Von Klown might be in the front office. But if we looked around, maybe we could find another way out. After all, we couldn't stay in the Haunted House forever!

I began tip-toeing down the hall, followed by Andy. We walked very, very slowly.

We went down a hall, through a dark room, then another hall. At the end of the hall, a light glowed through a window in the door.

Andy leaned forward, whispering. "I wonder if that's the office," he said.

We both stopped, listening for any sounds. We didn't hear anything.

"Maybe we can slip out the front after all," I said. "Maybe Klaus Von Klown isn't in his office. Maybe we can get out that way."

"It would be our lucky day," Andy replied, and we both crept cautiously toward the closed door.

When we were only a few feet away, we stopped again, listening for any sound.

Still nothing.

I took a couple of cautious steps forward, and peered through the window.

The minute I did, I gasped in shock. Andy saw my reaction and he crept forward, looking over my shoulder, peering through the window.

It was the front office, all right. Bright white light glowed from florescent tubes on the ceiling. On the far wall, the carnival activities were visible through a small window.

But it was the sight on the floor that caught my attention and made me gasp.

A desk had been turned over. A black leather chair was on its side. Papers were scattered about. It looked like a tornado had gone through.

But, by far, the most disturbing sight was the man in the corner of the room. He was tied to a folding chair, hands behind his back. His feet were tied together, and a small, fuzzy beanie-toy was stuffed in his mouth. The man was struggling to free himself, wriggling back and forth.

And I recognized the man instantly. The man was none other than Klaus Von Klown!

21

I turned the doorknob and opened the door. I think the movement must've surprised Klaus Von Klown, because he stopped squirming around and stared up at us in surprise.

"What happened?" Andy asked, but of course, Klaus Von Klown couldn't answer. He had a beanie-toy stuck in his mouth. He only mumbled and gagged.

I reached forward and pulled the small stuffed animal from his mouth. He took a sudden, deep breath.

"Thank you," he heaved, breathing heavily. "I can't thank you enough. Help me get untied."

Andy drew forward and knelt down and was going to begin working to free Klaus Von Klown.

"Not so fast," I said, placing my hand on Andy's shoulder. Andy stopped. "Not until you tell us what's going on here," I said.

"Fair enough," Klaus Von Klown said. His voice was tense. "It's the Klowns. My Klowns. I created them to be fun. To work here at the carnival. That's what I programmed them to do. But they've gotten way out of hand. I didn't think that it would go this far!"

"What would go this far?" I asked.

"The Klowns. And their plans. I created them to work. I didn't expect them to think. I didn't expect them to be this smart."

"So, they're all robots?" I asked.

Klaus Von Klown nodded, bobbing his head. "Yes," he explained. "Every last one of them. Just robots. I have programmed them with my voice, so they all sound like me."

So *that* was it! I was right! That's why all of the Klowns sounded the same! It was Klaus Von Klown's voice! Every robot had been programmed with his voice!

"But what about the green juice I found in the tent?" I asked.

Klaus Von Klown shook his head. "That's not juice," he answered. "That's battery acid. That's what powers the Klowns. They drink battery acid and eat old radio parts."

So that explained it! Earlier in the tent, the Klowns had been making sandwiches all right—but they sure weren't the kind of sandwiches that I'd want to eat!

"If we don't stop them," Klaus Von Klown continued, "they'll soon be much more intelligent that any human. They'll be able to think faster and better than anyone. There will be no stopping them. When I first made them, I called them 'Klaus Von Klown's Kooky Klowns.' They were supposed to be funny and make people laugh. Now, I think that 'Kreepy Klowns' might be more appropriate."

"How are they going to make themselves smarter?" I asked.

"The Klowns have intelligence, but they want more. They want to keep their computer chip brains, but they want to add the power of the human brain. They want to keep their own robot bodies, but they want the intelligence that can only be found in humans. The problem is, they've discovered a way to get it."

"How?" I asked. This whole story was getting weirder and weirder by the moment.

"It's in the gravitron ride," Klaus explained. "Although the Klowns aren't quite as smart as humans, they've created a machine within the gravitron that will transfer the brain waves from humans right into the computer chips in the Klowns. It will give each Klown the intelligence that they want. Each Klown will be smarter . . . much smarter than any single human. Then, there will be no stopping them."

"You mean," Andy began, "that the Klowns are going to kill people?"

Klaus Von Klown shook his head. "No, not kill them," he replied. "But they'll kill their minds and kill their memories. The people that are in the gravitron tonight will lose their minds. After the Klowns are finished, people won't remember friends or family. They won't remember who they are or where they live. They'll be like zombies for the rest of their lives."

I was about to ask something, but I forgot what it was. My thoughts were interrupted by a loud cheer from the crowd outside.

Oh no!

Across the midway on the other side of the festival site, a long line of people had formed. They were clapping and cheering, hands in the air.

It was the gravitron. All day it had sat motionless, with an 'opening soon' sign.

Now, the lights began to flash. The lights began to flash—and the gravitron began to turn!

22

It was a nightmare. This was not what I was expecting on my birthday, of all days.

All of those poor, unsuspecting people that were waiting in line had no idea what was waiting for them inside the gravitron.

"Hurry!" Klaus Von Klown urged. "Untie me! I must stop them!"

Andy and I went to work, loosening the tightly-knotted ropes that bound him to the chair. In less than a minute, he was free.

"How are you going to stop them?" Andy asked.

"I'm going to try to override the main power to the gravitron," Klaus Von Klown answered, quickly glancing out the window. The gravitron was lit up brightly, but the line of people hadn't begun to move. Soon, however, they would. Soon, the Klowns would begin to let people inside the gravitron.

"But what if that doesn't work?" I asked. "What then?"

Klaus Von Klown shook his head. "Then," he said, "it will be too late."

I didn't like the sound of that at all.

A large red toolbox sat next to a filing cabinet in the corner of the office. Klaus Von Klown hurried over to it and pulled out several tools, including a screwdriver, wire cutters, and some black electrical tape.

"You two stay here," he said. "It's too dangerous to be out there right now."

And with that, Klaus Von Klown opened up the front door and raced off. We saw him dart behind a row of trailers and over to a big metal utility shed.

"Do you think it will work?" I asked Andy.

"Who knows?" he said. "There's nothing we can do now except wait."

The feeling was awful. Here we were in Klaus Von Klowns office, while all of those people waited in line . . . waiting to go to their doom. They had no idea the fate that would meet them inside the gravitron.

Seconds ticked by. Then minutes. It seemed like hours were hurling along.

Still nothing. We kept waiting and watching, hoping to see the lights of the gravitron blink out. They never did.

Suddenly, another cheer rang out from the crowded line of people in front of the ride. Andy and I gasped in horror.

The gravitron had been warming up, but now it had stopped spinning! The door was opening!

Terror gripped me like a vice as the Klowns were letting people in.

"It's too late!" I cried. "The Klowns! They're letting people inside!"

We could see the smiling faces of adults and children as they made their way up the steel ramp to the gravitron. Some of them turned and waved to their friends or family. They had no idea that it would be the last time they would ever remember them, the last time they would know their name.

It was more than I could bear, watching all of those helpless people. We had to do something. We had to at least try.

Suddenly, I had an idea. It was a long shot, but it just might work.

"Kevin!" I shouted. "Put your clown mask on!"

"Huh?" he replied.

"Put your clown mask on! I have an idea!"

I sprang to Klaus Von Klown's desk. There was clown make-up, colored wigs, and different colored plastic noses scattered about.

I wasted no time. I looked into a mirror on the wall and frantically began to paint my face white. Then I made two huge, blue eyebrows, then a big red smile painted around my lips. I plopped an orange wig on my head and pinched a round plastic ball to my nose. I looked into the mirror.

Kinda messy and rushed, I thought. *But it might work. It just might work.*

"What's your idea?" Andy asked.

"There's an emergency exit on the other side of the gravitron," I began. "If we can sneak over to it and open it up from the outside, then we can tell the people on the inside that there's a problem with the ride, and they have to leave while it's being repaired. They'll believe us because they'll think we're clowns."

"And the Klowns will think we're one of them!" Andy said excitedly. "It might work!"

"Let's go!" I said, springing for the door.

We were off. The gravitron was on the other side of the carnival, and we had to weave in and out of the crowd.

Suddenly I was stopped by a hand that grasped my shoulder! It spun me around so hard that I almost fell.

It was a woman. A large woman, wearing a tie-dyed T-shirt, was holding a huge, pillow-sized bag of cotton candy in one hand. Next to her stood a wide-eyed small girl, maybe four or five years old. A camera dangled from a strap around the large woman's neck, and she reached for it.

"I've been trying to get a picture of my daughter with one of you clowns all day," she said hastily, snapping the lens cover from her camera. "You clowns are the rudest ones I've ever seen. In fact, I've been trying to find the person in charge of this place so I can complain."

"Well, ma'am," I explained, "he's been kind of tied-up lately."

It was true.

Andy had stopped, and he turned, standing a few feet away from me.

"Ma'am," I pleaded. "I'm really in a hurry. I've got to—"

"This'll just take a second," she interrupted. She gave a gentle nudge to her daughter. "Go on, sweetie-kins. Go stand next to the rude clown."

Reluctantly, the small girl left her mother's side and cautiously walked up to me.

I turned and looked anxiously over at the gravitron. Andy was watching it, too. People were still walking up the metal ramp. I kept hoping to see the lights blink out, to see the large dish-like ride stop spinning, but it didn't. It just whirred around like a fat top. It wouldn't be long now.

Pop!

A bright light flashed, and I turned to face the

woman with the camera.

"Aww," she began, lowering the camera and advancing the film with her thumb. She looked at her daughter. "That silly clown wasn't looking. We'll have to take another one."

"Please hurry," I said. "I really have to —"

"Oh, clowns aren't in any rush," she interrupted again. "I promised my daughter a picture with a clown. So far, you're the only one who has even spoken to us. So just hold your horses for another second."

Of all the luck, I thought.

"Kayleigh!" Andy shouted from behind me. I wanted to turn and answer him, but I was afraid that if I did, the large woman would snap a picture right at that moment. Then we'd have to take another one.

I swallowed hard and tried to smile.

Pop!

The flash lit up the surrounding area and faded quickly.

"There," the woman said, advancing the film again and placing the cover back over the lens. "That wasn't so bad, was it?"

"Enjoy the rides," I said, turning and walking quickly away.

Yikes! That was exactly what that awful Klown

had said to me earlier. His voice came back to me, churning through my head like a roller coaster.

I shook his voice away and caught up with Andy. In the distance, more and more people were climbing up the steel plank, disappearing into the huge red dome.

"We've got to hurry!" I shouted above the crowd noise.

We made a loop around the Ferris wheel so we could approach the gravitron from the opposite side. There weren't many people over there, and we didn't see any Klowns.

But we did see one thing that gave me hope. Granted, it was only a flicker of hope, but it was all I had.

A large, glowing EMERGENCY EXIT sign shined brightly above a steel door. The door was ten feet off the ground, but metal steps led all the way down to the ground.

The gravitron continued to hum loudly, and its lights shined brightly above us. I had been hoping to see the whole thing shut down, to hear the huge motors slowly whir to a stop, due to a lack of power. I'd hoped that Klaus Von Klown had been successful in his attempt to cut the electricity.

Those hopes faded. The gravitron engines

roared, as powerful as ever.

If the people inside the ride were going to be saved, it was going to be up to us.

And our only hope was getting them out through the emergency exit.

Andy and I bounded up the metal stairs. Our feet clanged on the rickety steps, but we didn't even notice. We were too concerned with getting to the emergency exit.

At the top of the stairs, I had a horrible thought.

What if the emergency door wouldn't open? What if it would only open from the inside?

I reached for the doorknob, hoping . . . .

Yes! The knob turned in my hand and the door began to open! It squeaked loudly as it swung outward.

Inside, the walls of the gravitron were lined with excited people. They were all waiting impatiently for everyone to be inside, and for the ride to start.

We wasted no time.

"Sorry folks," Andy shouted loudly, cupping his hands around his mouth. The crowd began to quiet down. "There's a problem with the gravitron. Everybody off. We'll have the problem fixed soon."

A loud groan swept through the crowd inside the gravitron. Andy and I stepped away from the door, and, reluctantly, people began filing by us! It was working! They were leaving the gravitron!

"Sorry folks," I said, as people continued past. I could see the disappointment in their faces.

If only they knew!

"Keep coming, folks," Andy said loudly. "Problems with the gravitron. We'll have it fixed soon."

I kept wanting to urge the people along faster, but I couldn't. They were moving out the emergency exit and down the metal stairs as fast as they safely could.

Inside the gravitron, the crowd of people had grown much smaller. Soon, the ride was empty.

It worked! We had stopped the Klowns and their vicious plan to steal the brain waves from innocent people!

"Let's get out of here," Andy said. We both spun and were about to head down the steps — but we didn't get far.

Because the Klowns were blocking our way out.

25

Two of them. They were bounding up the metal steps of the emergency exit, cutting off our escape route.

And they were not amused.

Thinking quick, I reached out and pulled the emergency door shut. It slammed closed just in time, and Andy turned the bolt lock just as the Klowns on the other side had grasped the knob. We could hear them pulling at the door, trying to get it open, but they were too late.

My heart soared and my hope grew . . . but not

for long—because on the other side of the gravitron, the main door was sliding shut! We didn't even have time to take a single step before it had slammed closed.

We were trapped. We were trapped in the gravitron.

"This really isn't looking very good," Andy said.

"No kidding," I said sarcastically. "Come on. We've got to find a way out of here."

We began searching the inside of the gravitron for another door. Somewhere, there had to be another exit or entrance. Maybe a small trap door that would lead to the motor room.

We searched and searched. We went over every inch of the inside, every crack and cranny.

No doors. There was no other way in . . . and no other way out.

We were prisoners, but that wasn't the most horrifying part. The most horrifying part was that we were trapped inside the gravitron . . . the terrible machine that the Klowns would use to steal our brains.

My mind was spinning a billion miles a second, trying to think of a way out. Thoughts raced at breakneck speed.

Then—horror. A terror swept though my body like I had never felt before. I could feel movement. The gravitron had started to spin.

A tight knot formed in my stomach. It twisted and turned and felt like a rock. A lump formed in my throat. It felt like a baseball.

"*Oh no!*" I screamed over the churning motor of the gravitron. "Now *we're* trapped!"

It sure wasn't looking good.

"We'll be all right if we stay on the metal walkway," Andy said loudly. "Remember . . . the machine works only when people are pinned against the wall by the force of the gravitron spinning around."

It was true. Maybe if we stayed on the walkway, we'd be okay.

No such luck. In the next instant, the catwalk below us began to slowly fall away, exposing a deep dark, bottomless pit! There was no place else to go . . . except to the walls of the spinning gravitron.

I leapt off the walkway just in time. If I would have stood there a moment longer, I would have fallen. Andy had already done the same, but now our backs were leaning up against the wall of the spinning machine . . . which was going faster by the second.

This was it. We were done. There was no way out of this now. The gravitron kept spinning faster and faster, and the roaring of the motor was deafening. The faster the gravitron spun, the more difficult it became to even move.

A computer screen in the center of the gravitron began to flash. I hadn't noticed it before, since I had been paying too much attention on getting the people out. But there was a big computer screen in the center of the machine. As we spun around it, I could read the huge letters:

please wait: achieving maximum beta wave

brain transfer speed

The letters began to blink.

"*I think this is it for us!*" I shouted to Andy. "*I'm sorry I got you into this!*"

"*It's not your fault!*" Andy shouted above the awful roar. "*I would have come to the carnival anyway!*"

The gravitron began to spin even faster, and the feeling of being smooshed against the wall was almost unbearable. I've been in gravitrons before, but I've never been in one that went so fast.

I felt dizzy, and things began to look fuzzy. I caught a glimpse of the computer screen as we spun madly around it. It was hard to read, because we were moving so fast. Plus, the letters on the screen were blinking. But there was no mistaking what they read:

maximum beta wave brain transfer speed achieved

I felt like I was going to barf. The speed of the gravitron, the dizziness in my head, plus the fear of what was about to happen was almost too much. Everything got real fuzzy and I felt lightheaded.

"Good-bye Andy," I managed to say, but I know he didn't hear me. I was too weak to shout it out, and the force of the twirling gravitron was too strong to fight anymore.

And then, everything went black.

So this was what it was like to lose your brain.

Black. Nothing but black.

But wait a minute.

I could *still* hear the gravitron whirring loudly—*only it was slowing down!* I . . . I could still think! I remembered that my name is Kayleigh, and it was my birthday, and that I lived in Kalamazoo, Michigan.

Had my brain been stolen? Had I lost my mind?

No! There was some other reason for the blackness. There had to be.

"Andy!" I shouted above the drone of the gravitron. Even now, the motor seemed to be slowing rapidly.

"I'm right here," he said. He was right next to me in the darkness, but it was impossible to see him.

Suddenly, I knew! I knew what had happened!

"Klaus Von Klown!" I said excitedly. "He must've been able to kill the power to the gravitron!"

"And just in time, too," Andy said. "I thought my brain was gone for sure."

We had to think fast. The whirling gravitron was slowing down quickly, but there was no floor below us. Just a thin edge along the sides of the wall.

That would have to do. Somehow, we would have to walk along the tiny edge and find one of the doors.

We'd worry about the Klowns then.

"I think the closest door is this way," I said, turning to my right. "Over here."

I crept carefully along the edge of the gravitron, the tips of my toes clinging to the small ledge that was our only footing. It was scary, walking along like that, not knowing where we were going. I kept my hands along the metal wall, sweeping up and down and back and forth, trying to find the door.

"Anything yet?" Andy asked from behind me.

"No," I answered. It sure was frustrating. Plus, I knew that any minute the Klowns would storm the gravitron, looking for us.

It wasn't a pleasant thought.

Then, the absolute worst thing imaginable happened. I had been trying to be extra careful to keep my footing—but I slipped.

I slipped . . . and I fell. I fell, sliding down the wall, tumbling blindly through total darkness.

I think you can imagine the terror I felt, falling, not knowing where I was falling to, not able to see a single thing.

And then—*smack!* I hit the ground!

I tumbled head long and landed on my face, hitting my nose and chin on the ground. I could tell it was the ground, too. I could feel the cool grass beneath me, the damp dew on my cheeks.

And I could see cracks of light! I was beneath the gravitron! I could hear music from the carnival, and the distant laughs and shouts of people.

"Andy!" I shouted up into the darkness. "It's okay! I'm fine! Slide off the ledge!"

"Where are you?!?!" he shouted from the darkness above.

"I'm right below you!" I answered. "It's okay! I think we can find our way out!"

Suddenly I could hear a swishing sound, and then I was knocked to the ground again.

"*Oooooooof!*" I gasped as the wind was knocked out of me.

Andy had smacked right into me!

"Hey, I guess that wasn't so bad after all," he said.

"Yeah," I said, not hiding my disgust. "That's because you landed on *me!*"

He stood up, and I did the same. We were still in the dark, still beneath the gravitron.

"Look over there," I said. I pointed to some of the slivers of light that I saw. "We should be able to get out of here."

We walked slowly through the darkness, wary of any metal beams or pipes that might be protruding out. Thankfully, there were none.

I crouched down and peered out one of the cracks. I could see the carnival, still in full swing.

Everyone seemed unaware of what was going on inside the gravitron.

"Hey," Andy said, feeling the tin wall. "This is just aluminum skirting, like a pop can," he said. "We should be able to bend this and get out of here."

He was right. The skirting underneath the gravitron was just cheap, thin aluminum. Andy grabbed the bottom of it and pulled, succeeding in bending it upward. The metal creaked and crinkled. When the opening was big enough for each of us to slip through, he stopped.

We both crouched low to the ground, checking out the carnival around us. The last thing we wanted was to run into any more Klowns!

The sun was setting, and the sky beyond the Arcadia Festival Site was turning brilliant shades of pink and orange. The sky above us was growing dark, and the lights of the carnival rides glowed brightly.

The only Klowns we could see stood by the opening of the main gate. They were allowing people in, but no one appeared to be leaving. I counted four Klowns standing by the gate.

"Let's make a break for it," Andy whispered after we didn't see any Klowns close by. "Maybe we can make it back to Klaus Von Klown's office."

What we would do then, I hadn't a clue, but it seemed like a safer place than hanging out beneath the gravitron.

Andy was first. He wriggled beneath the aluminum, crawled forward, then leapt to his feet.

"Hurry!" he whispered to me.

I crawled on the grass and pulled myself through. My shoulder caught on a piece of the metal and tore my shirt.

"Ouch!" I hissed. When I looked, I saw a faint trickle of red dotting my shoulder, but I didn't have time to attend to the wound now. Besides, I hadn't cut myself very bad. I'd take care of it later.

Right now I just wanted to make a beeline to Klaus Von Klown's office and lock the doors!

We ran down the midway and in front of the concession stands.

So far, so good.

We wound around a few rides. I could see Klaus Von Klown's office in the distance, and the dark shape of the Haunted House looming beyond.

We were going to make it.

Keep running, I said to myself. *Just keep running, Kayleigh.*

I kept waiting for a Klown to leap out from a crowd of people and grab me, but none did. It was almost with surprise that I found ourselves safely at Klaus Von Klown's office.

Andy grabbed the knob and the door sprang open, and I slammed it closed as soon as we were both safe inside, locking it behind me.

Whew! We made it.

Andy sprinted to the back door that led into the Haunted House and he shut it, locking it tight. I could hear the bolts rattle as he tested it.

Safe. It was the safest I'd felt all day.

Until I heard a noise and turned—and saw the face of Klaus Von Klown! He'd been hiding in a closet, and he came toward me carrying two wires connected to something!

"It's too late," he said. "Your plan isn't going to work. This is the end for you!"

Suddenly, I realized what was going on!

I still looked like a Klown! I was still wearing make-up and a wig and a plastic nose! Klaus Von Klown thought that I was one of them!

"Mr. Von Klown!" I shouted, pulling the wig from my head. "It's me! It's *us!*"

Klaus Von Klown stopped. He had a puzzled look on his face. He dropped his hands and held the wires at his side.

"Goodness," he said. "I thought you were

149

robots! I almost electrocuted you!"

"You were able to kill the power to the gravitron!" Andy exclaimed. "It worked!"

"Not for long, I'm afraid," Klaus Von Klown said, shaking his head. "The Klowns are pretty smart. They'll be able to fix the problem soon. But if we hurry, maybe we can get people out of the carnival."

But in the next instant, we realized that it might even be too late for that—because on the other side of the carnival, the lights of the gravitron blinked. They went on and off a couple times, then stayed on.

The Klowns were already at work.

"Come on!" Klaus Von Klown said. "We can try one more thing. We might be able to short-circuit the gravitron for good!"

Klaus Von Klown turned and sprang to the door . . . but there were three Klowns waiting for us outside! They began pounding on the window, trying to get in!

"The back door!" Andy shouted, pointing toward the back of the office with his arm. "Can we make it out through the Haunted House by using the back door?!?!"

"We'll have to try!" Klaus Von Klown replied. "Come on! Hurry!"

We followed him to the back door of the office.

He quickly unbolted the lock and flung the door open. I was right on his heels, and Andy followed, pulling the door closed behind him.

We ran down the hall and through a darkened room, then turned down another dark hall. The inside of the Haunted House was like a maze. There was just barely enough light to see in the halls. I imagine that when the Haunted House was open with all of its displays, it was probably pretty scary.

All of a sudden, a loud *crack!* filled the air, and everything went black! We were in the dark. I felt like I was in the coffin again, only I was standing up.

We were in complete darkness.

The three of us stopped. Without any lights on, it was impossible to see.

"Terrific," Andy said. I couldn't see him, but his voice was close by. "Next time I come to a carnival, I'm bringing a flashlight."

"I think the Klowns have cut off power to the Haunted House," Klaus Von Klown said. "They know we're in here, and they know it'll be difficult for us to get out if we can't see."

"How difficult?" I asked.

"Difficult . . . but not impossible," Klaus Von Klown answered. "The main thing is, we have to stick together. Come on."

I followed his footsteps in the dark, and we wound through rooms and hallways. I bumped into a wall here and there, and Andy bumped into me a couple times. Once I bumped into something that felt furry. I jumped, but then I realized we were in the hall with all of the wax figures.

But Klaus Von Klown was right. After a few minutes, he stopped.

"Ah-ha," he said. I heard keys jingling. "We made it."

I was relieved to hear him say that. We had found the back door. It was locked from the inside, but Klaus Von Klown had a key. In a moment, the door was open.

"Hold on a minute," he said, bending down and peering out the crack of the open door. "I'm going to make sure they're not waiting for us."

After a few anxious moments, Klaus Von Klown decided that all was clear.

But one look toward the other side of the carnival told us that it might already be too late.

Because the gravitron was spinning madly, whirling like a frantic, glowing top.

30

"No!" Klaus shouted. "We can't let them do this!"

But the situation seemed hopeless. The gravitron was whirling like crazy, and I didn't see how we would be able to stop the Klowns now.

Klaus Von Klown turned quickly, glancing at Andy, then me. "Run to the gravitron!" he ordered. "Run to the gravitron and find the main power accelerator! It will be right below the door. But be careful! There will be Klowns all around. When you see the power go out on all of the other rides, turn the main power accelerator on the gravitron to 'high'."

"But won't that just give the ride more power?" I asked.

"Yes," Klaus Von Klown answered, nodding his head. "But if we give it *too much* power, it might just overload the gravitron's engines. The idea is to shut that thing down for good."

I hoped he knew what he was doing.

"Go! Now!" Klaus Von Klown directed, and he immediately took off running the other direction.

"Come on, Andy!" I shouted.

Once again we were off, running through the crowd of people. It was still amazing to me that no one else at the carnival had any idea what was going on with the Klowns or the gravitron. Everyone was caught up in the excitement of the moment, playing games, eating carnival food, and having fun.

If they only knew.

At the gravitron, Klaus Von Klown was right. There were Klowns everywhere—but they all were seated in a row around the gravitron. All of them had some strange device with coiled wires hooked to their heads.

And they were all smiling. Not nice smiles, but real strange smirks that made you think that they were getting away with something.

Not if we could help it.

Andy and I stopped near the cotton candy booth, watching.

"There," Andy said, pointing.

Below the door of the spinning gravitron was a control booth. There was no one near it. I think all of the Klowns were hooked to the strange apparatus that connected them to the gravitron.

All at once, the carnival lights went dim. The rides began to slow, and a wave of disappointment swept through the crowd. The power didn't go completely out, but almost. All of the lights on the rides were still lit, but they weren't nearly as bright as they had been.

"Now!" I said to Andy. We ran across the midway to the gravitron, not stopping until we reached the control panel. The gravitron was really moving now, and I thought that we might already be too late.

We grabbed the metal bar with both hands and tried to pull it up. It moved. Just a little, but it moved.

"Harder!" I shouted to Andy. "We've got to try harder!"

We pulled and pulled. The lever wouldn't budge any more. It seemed like it was stuck in one position.

Above us, the gravitron whirled on. We could hear the excited shrieks of the people inside, having the time of their lives.

We weren't too late . . . yet. But if we couldn't get the power lever to move—

Suddenly, the lever gave in. In one quick motion, it slid into the 'high' position. The sudden, quick movement caught us off guard, and Andy and I tumbled backward, falling to the ground.

But it worked!

The lights of the gravitron grew real bright for a moment—but suddenly, there was a loud popping sound from the engines.

The whirring gravitron began to slow down! I could hear the engine start to whine, and the entire ride was slowing. I hoped we weren't too late.

But even more bizarre were the Klowns. They were all still seated, connected to the strange contraptions, when all at once, they all began to shake! Each Klown had a look of horror on his face. Sparks began to fly from the units connected to their heads. The Klowns began to bounce violently in their chairs, shaking uncontrollably.

One by one . . . the Klowns exploded! Sparks and wires went everywhere, and the robot Klowns

156

became nothing more than a tangled mess of burning wires. It was the freakiest thing I'd ever seen. The robots, their circuits overloaded with electricity, blew up like big firecrackers, showering the area with sparks. It was crazy.

In less than a minute, all of the Klowns were gone. History. There was nothing left of them except a mass of smoldering wires and metal. They didn't even look like clowns anymore. Just old pieces of burned equipment.

The lights of the other rides began to glow brighter, and once again a cheer rolled through the crowd. The Ferris wheel began to spin, bells and whistles could be heard, and things began to return to normal.

The gravitron stopped spinning and the door opened up. People filed out with big smiles on their faces, but it was obvious that their brains were still intact. The Klowns hadn't succeeded with their plan.

Klaus Von Klown came running across the midway, snapping his head around, glancing nervously at the people leaving the gravitron.

"Did it work?" he asked anxiously. "Did it work?"

I nodded my head and pointed to the row of cooked wires. Klaus Von Klown rushed over to what was left of his Klowns. He inspected each robot carefully.

"Thank goodness," he said. "If they would have succeeded, there would have been no stopping them." He walked over to the entrance of the gravitron and pulled a chain across the doorway, and placed the 'closed' sign in front. He walked back over to where we were.

"I can't thank you enough," he said, shaking our hands. "You saved the day. I don't know how I can repay you."

"No problem," Andy said. "But if you wouldn't mind, I'd kind of like to go hit some of the rides. We haven't had a chance to do that very much."

"Of course!" Klaus Von Klown said. "That's it! For the rest of the week, you and all of your friends can come to the carnival and ride all of the rides you want . . . *for free.*"

Wow! What a reward! This week was going to be a riot!

"Gee, thanks!" Andy replied.

"Yeah, thanks!" I said. "Thanks a lot!"

It was like getting an extra-special birthday present.

We played a few of the games and went on

some of the rides. I had a lot of fun . . . now that I didn't have to worry about the Klowns. I sure was glad they were gone.

Andy and I stuck together for the rest of the evening. We ran into a few friends, but we didn't bother to tell them about the Klowns. There was a lot to tell, and besides . . . everybody was here for fun. They didn't want to hear about robot Klowns and gravitrons that sucked all the intelligence from your brain.

We rode a few more rides, then it was time to go home. Andy and I walked by Klaus Von Klown's office and waved good-bye, then left through the main gate. I looked back over my shoulder at the bustling activity.

And we get to ride for free all week, I thought excitedly. *What fun!*

Everything had turned out okay, after all. I was fine, Andy was fine, nobody got hurt. We had stopped the awful robots before they could go through with their terrible plan. I was sure I wouldn't be seeing any more clowns.

I was wrong.

31

We walked home under the white glow of the streetlights. Soon, the sights and sounds from the carnival faded off into the night. I took one last glance back at the Arcadia Festival Site, admiring the beautiful, neon-colored lights of the carnival.

I had a funny feeling as we walked along the sidewalk. It was getting late. Lights were on in a few homes, and there were kids playing in their yards. Laughter came from backyards, and every once in a while I caught the scent of barbeque drifting in the night air.

But I had a strange feeling. I had a feeling that I was being watched.

"Do . . . do you notice anything strange?" I asked Andy quietly.

He turned his head, glancing at the rows of houses. "No," he replied. "Like what?"

"I don't know," I answered. "But I get the feeling that we're being watched."

"It's just your imagination," he said.

He was probably right. At night, I can get spooked easily. I can't help it.

But I was glad that Andy was with me — especially when we turned and rounded the last corner on our block.

Our house sat at the end of the court, completely dark. All of the other homes had lights on . . . except ours.

Andy noticed it, too. "That's strange," he said. "The porch light isn't even on."

Mom and Dad always leave the porch light on when we're out. *Always.*

As we drew closer, it was obvious that no one was home.

That's crazy, I thought. *Where would Mom and Dad go? They were always home when we came home.*

We stopped at the foot of the drive, staring up at our dark house. Nothing moved, and the house looked cold and empty.

"Come on," Andy said. "Mom and Dad probably got tired and went to bed. Or maybe Dad fell asleep watching TV, and Mom turned the lights off and went to bed."

That's another thing about Andy. He is optimistic . . . he usually thinks that things can't be as bad as they seem, and he always believes that things will work out fine.

I always try and look at the bright side of things too . . . but while I was staring at our dark house, I wasn't so sure.

Andy began walking up the dark driveway, and I followed. Up the porch steps, across the deck . . . and to the front door.

Andy grabbed the knob and the door slowly began to chug open.

I held my breath.

Inside, the house was completely dark. Nothing moved, not a sound was heard.

Andy was first to go in, and I followed, closing the door behind me. I wasted no time in flicking the switch.

Light exploded, illuminating the entire room.

But it was what was in the kitchen that caught my attention.

I froze in terror, and my blood ran cold. My spine turned to ice and I stood motionless, unable to do anything.

There, in the doorway of the kitchen, stood a clown.

32

"SURPRISE!"

The unexpected shout startled me, and I jumped. Suddenly, people began popping out from everywhere . . . from behind couches, chairs, closets . . . soon the room was filled with people!

"Happy birthday, Kayleigh!" everyone shouted, clapping their hands and cheering. My face turned eight shades of red.

The clown in the kitchen came toward me, holding a bouquet of balloons that read 'happy birthday'. He leaned down and gave me a hug.

"Happy birthday, sweetheart," he said.

I'd know that voice anywhere!

It was Dad! Dad had dressed up like a clown for my birthday!

Andy was looking at me, smirking. I could tell from the way he was giggling that he knew about the surprise party all along. I just laughed and shook my head.

A surprise birthday party. I should have known.

We had cake and ice cream and pop, and then I got to open presents. I got some really cool clothes and even some CDs. It was a lot of fun.

But best of all, a lot of my friends were there. Some of them I hadn't seen in a long time. Even Nicholas Spencer was there. Nick had been one of my very best friends up until last year. Then he moved to somewhere near Detroit, and I hadn't seen him since. We e-mail each other now and then, but I still miss him.

We talked for a long time. He told me about their new house, and that he liked his new school and new friends.

"Man, you should have seen your face when the lights came on!" he said, munching on a piece of birthday cake. His smile grew wide. "You looked like you'd seen a ghost!"

"Well, that's because I just had a bad experience with a bunch of Klowns," I said. "And that's 'Klowns' with a 'K'."

He looked at me strangely. "Well," he said, "I just had a bad experience with dinosaurs. That's 'dinosaurs' with a capital 'D'."

"Dinosaurs?" I asked. "What are you talking about?"

"Did you hear about the dinosaurs that were spotted in Detroit last summer?"

"How could I forget?" I answered. Everybody knew about the strange dinosaurs that had suddenly attacked the city of Detroit. It was totally crazy.

"Well, don't tell anybody, but I was responsible for that whole mess," Nick said.

"What?!?!?" I exclaimed, my eyes bulging. "You?!?!? How?!?!"

"How much time have we got?" he asked, popping another piece of birthday cake into his mouth. "This might take a while . . . ."

NEXT IN THE 'MICHIGAN CHILLERS'
SERIES:

DINOSAURS

DESTROY

DETROIT

**Continue reading for a few sample
chapters!**

I've always thought it would be great to travel through time. To go back and see what happened during some particular era, or even go into the future to see what it would be like a thousand years from now.

But when my grandpa said that once, every fifty years, you could do just that — using a window through time — I didn't believe him. I thought he was just telling me a story.

Grandpa said that once every fifty years, on

June 28th, at exactly 3:05 in the afternoon, a window through time would open up. A window that would allow a person to step through and travel in time, but only for a period of seven days. He said that the window was in a field not far from where I lived. His father had told him about it, and his father before him. That's how he knew about it.

Yeah, right. Like I was going to believe *that*.

But on June 28th of this year, at exactly 3:05 in the afternoon, I found out that my grandpa hadn't been trying to fool me. Because my friend Summer and I found the window in time . . . and what followed set off a chain of events that the city of Detroit wouldn't soon forget.

On the morning of Monday, June 28th, I was awakened by the lawnmower outside. Dad was working in the yard, and so was Mom. Dad works overnights at the factory, so he gets home at about eight in the morning and usually goes to work in the yard for a while before he goes to bed. Once a week he mows the lawn, and this was one of those mornings. When that mower fires up, it's no use trying to sleep any more. It sounds like the space shuttle taking off.

But I suddenly remembered something: today was Monday.

Not just any Monday.

It was Monday, the 28th of June. This was the day Grandpa said that the window through time would open.

That is, of course, if there even was such a thing — and if I could find it.

I got dressed and sat down in the kitchen for a quick breakfast. The phone rang while I was eating a bowl of *Froot Loops*.

"Hello?" I said, picking up the receiver.

"Nick . . . it's Summer. Are we still going today?"

Summer McCready is one of my best friends. She was one of the first people I met when I moved to Detroit, and she's pretty cool. We go to the same school and ride the same bus. Yesterday, I told her about the window through time. She didn't laugh like I thought she would.

In fact, she looked fascinated.

"Let's go find it!" she'd said excitedly. I told her to call me in the morning, and we'd make plans.

"You bet we're still going!" I answered,

chomping on my cereal. "Otherwise, we won't have another chance for fifty years."

"Do you really think it's true?" she asked.

"I don't know," I pondered. "I asked my dad, and he just laughed. He said that Grandpa had told him about the window, but he didn't believe it. He never went to look for it."

My excitement was growing by the second, but so was my fear.

What if we really found the window? Would we travel back in time? Would we travel forward? That would be cool!

Either way, I was more than willing to spend an afternoon trying to find the window through time.

We agreed to meet at one o'clock at a corner store that wasn't far from my house. From there, we would ride our bikes to find the field that Grandpa talked about.

I got to the store just before one, and went inside. I bought a coke for each of us, along with a couple Slim Jims.

And a camera. One of those disposable ones that they sell for a few dollars. If there really was such a thing as a 'window through time' I wanted to have pictures of what we saw.

Summer showed up right on time, as usual.

We biked for miles . . . through neighborhoods, down strange streets, past tall buildings. I know my grandpa said that the field wasn't far from where I lived, but man . . . I think we biked ten miles!

Just before three o'clock, we found the field that my grandpa was talking about.

It was just like he'd said. The field was strewn with large rocks and old junk that had been placed there long ago. The rusted-out shell of an old car sat alone like a huge steel skeleton. On the south end of the field stood a large clump of trees. The trees were big . . . much bigger than Grandpa had described them. But I guess you'd expect them to be, since grandpa hadn't seen them in fifty years.

That was where the window through time was supposed to open up. Within the stand of trees at the south end of the field.

There was too much debris strewn through the field to ride our bikes, so we walked, pushing them alongside.

When we reached the shade of the trees, we stopped. Summer's long blonde hair swept gently in the light afternoon breeze.

"What are we supposed to be looking for?" she asked.

"I'm not really sure," I said. "My grandpa said

that it was just a big—"

Had I been able to finish my sentence, I would have said the words 'shimmering window'.

But I didn't get the chance to finish what I was saying . . . because right before us, at exactly 3:05, a thundering roar tore through the sky. It was the screeching sound of metal on metal, and it was *loud*.

Summer cupped her hands over her ears, and I did the same. I was shocked by the sudden noise—but it was nothing compared to the shock I received when I saw what was happening in the air right before my eyes.

Right before us, the window appeared. It opened like a nightshade, sweeping down toward the ground. It was about twenty feet wide and very high . . . taller than a house. It was as if a fuzzy gray sheet had been placed in the air right in front of us.

Then the grayness faded, giving way to a shimmering, clear window. I could see right through it! However, objects on the other side of the window — tree trunks, leaves, branches — they seemed to sway and bend. It was like looking at something through wavering heat waves.

I couldn't speak. My mouth was open, but I didn't know what to say. The noise had stopped, and all we could hear were a few birds chirping, and the sounds of the city in the distance.

The sun beamed down, and a trickle of sweat dripped down my forehead. I reached up and swept it away.

"Oh my gosh," Summer whispered. *"It's here! It's really here!"*

The window shimmered in front of us.

Did we dare? Should we step through?

I could think of a million reasons why we shouldn't.

But I could think of a *billion* reasons why we *should*.

"You wanna do this?" I asked quietly.

Summer turned her head and looked at me. "What do you think?" she asked. Her voice was soft, and maybe a bit fearful. Now that we had discovered that my grandpa was right—that there really *was* a window—we weren't too sure about the whole idea of time travel.

"Let's try," I said, nodding my head. "You hold onto my hand, and I'll step through. If there's a problem, you can pull me back. Simple."

Summer looked at the shimmering window, then turned and looked at me.

"Okay," she said. "Let's try it."

I took a step toward the window, and Summer followed. She held her hand out, and I took it in mine.

"If I squeeze your hand really hard, pull me back," I said. She nodded, understanding.

"Good luck," she said.

I turned and faced the strange, wavering window, took a deep breath . . . and stepped through.

I'm not sure what I expected, but I'll tell you what: there was nothing I could have imagined that would have prepared me for what I saw.

I found myself in a jungle! The air was thick and humid, and the sky was overcast and gray. Enormous ferns grew close by, and giant trees with wide, thick leaves towered above me. I could hear a creek babbling not far off.

And a volcano! Miles away, I could see a smoking volcano, spewing out black smoke into the

179

sky.

Where had I traveled to? Had I traveled back in time . . . or forward?

In two seconds, I had my answer, and it came from out of the sky. I heard a loud screech, and suddenly a gigantic bird appeared! It was far bigger than any other bird I had seen before. It looked like a small plane coasting over the treetops.

Wait a minute! I thought. *That's not a bird at all! That's . . . that's a flying reptile! It's a Quetzalcoatlus! I know it is!*

A Quetzalcoatlus is a winged reptile that lived during the Cretaceous period, about 65 million years ago. They're huge, with wingspan of nearly 40 feet. It is the largest flying animal ever discovered. I learned all about them when we studied dinosaurs in science class.

The giant, winged beast flew overhead, finally disappearing in the thick trees.

Wow! I had traveled back in time 65 million years! Back to the land of dinosaurs!

I was still holding Summer's hand. When I turned to see her, I got a surprise.

The window looked the same on this side as it did on the other! I could see trees and ferns on the other side, but they seemed to waver back and forth.

Summer was nowhere to be found.

I looked at my hand.

It was gone! It had vanished just above my wrist!

Where my hand met the window, it disappeared. Like I had dipped my hand into a pool of gray water!

But I could still feel Summer's tight grasp. I pulled, wanting her to come through. She had to see this.

I could feel her resisting. I think that maybe she was trying to pull me back, but I wanted her to see what I was seeing. She just *had* to see this!

I pulled with all my might. Suddenly, she came tumbling through the window. I lost my balance and I fell, and she came crashing down on top of me.

"I thought you were in trouble!" she exclaimed, standing up and brushing herself off. "I thought that—"

When she noticed where she was, she stopped speaking, not finishing her sentence. Her mouth hung open like a dead fish, and her eyes swirled about as she took in the strange surroundings.

"It's . . . it's . . . ." she stammered. She was too stunned to speak.

"It's the age of dinosaurs!" I finished for her. "We traveled back in time, millions and millions of years!"

We stared for a long, long time. Neither of us moved. Strange, animal-like sounds came from the thick jungle. It was all too bizarre, too unreal to even believe. I have seen paintings and drawings of what scientists believe the dinosaur era was like, but this was just too far out to even imagine.

"Come on," I said finally, taking a few steps toward a clump of ferns.

"Where are you going?" Summer asked, her voice filled with astonishment.

"I just want to go and check this place out a little more. Come on."

"What if we get lost?" she asked. "What then?"

She had a point. We couldn't wander too far from the window, or we might not be able to find our way back to it. Then, we'd never make it back through time. Dad would ground me for a month.

Wait a minute, I thought. *If we never made it back, how could Dad ground me?*

Either way, it wasn't a pleasant thought.

"We'll stay close by, I promise," I assured Summer. "Come on." I extended my hand toward her, and she reluctantly began walking toward me.

"Okay," she said. "But let's not go far."

As fate would have it, we wouldn't get very far at all.

We hadn't taken more than ten steps when we heard a loud noise in front of us. It was the sound of crunching branches and limbs.

Summer and I ducked behind a thick stand of small trees. The noise grew louder, and the heavy snapping and crunching drew closer. We nestled into the leaves, hoping that we were hidden.

Suddenly, we saw it, and I gasped out loud.

A dinosaur!

It was only twenty feet from us—and it was HUGE!

But what was even stranger: I recognized the beast!

"It's a Triceratops!" I whispered to Summer. *"I've seen them in my dinosaur books!"*

"Great," Summer replied. *"At least you know what kind of dinosaur we're going to be eaten by!"*

I shook my head. *"No,"* I said. *"The Triceratops is a plant-eater. They don't eat meat."*

"Let's hope so," Summer said.

Triceratops is a cool-looking dinosaur. They have three horns that protrude from their face, and a large, bony plate behind the back of its skull. One short horn is perched above the dinosaur's bird-like beak, and two longer ones that stick out just above the creature's eyes. They walk on four strong, thick legs. Triceratops looks like a huge rhinoceros.

We watched the creature as it continued slowly on its path. It didn't pay any attention to us. It acted as though we weren't even there.

I quickly thrust my hand into my pocket and pulled out my disposable camera. I hurriedly clicked off a couple of pictures of the Triceratops.

All of a sudden, the huge dinosaur stopped — and chewed on some leaves!

"See?" I said quietly. *"Just plants. I don't think that he'll hurt us."*

I was right, of course. The Triceratops wouldn't hurt us.

What I didn't know was that there was a creature sneaking up behind us at that very moment that *could* hurt us.

And I was about to know the real meaning of fear . . . because we were about to come face-to-face with a Tyrannosaurus Rex.

4

The Triceratops was moving away when we heard a noise behind us. It was a long, deliberate crunch, like something heavy was moving slowly through the brush.

Like it was stalking something.

I turned, and the sight behind me almost made me faint.

The beast towering above us was unmistakable. I'd seen drawings before, and I'd seen the movie *Jurassic Park*.

A Tyrannosaurus Rex.

I knew we were in deep trouble.

Summer turned, and when she saw the terrible beast looming over us, she screamed. I quickly grabbed her arm and told her to stop, that maybe the T-Rex couldn't see us, but she would have none of that. She jumped up and did the worst possible thing she could do.

She ran.

"Summer!" I shouted. *"Stop! Stop!"*

But it was too late. She had already sprang from our hiding place.

Not knowing what else to do, and thinking that the huge dinosaur had probably spotted us, I jumped up and ran after her.

Behind me, the T-Rex let out a terrible, loud screech. Trees snapped like toothpicks as the terrible beast began charging after us.

The problem was, he was attacking from behind us — cutting off our way back to the window through time! We were trapped!

"Nick!" Summer shouted from in front of me. "A cave! There's a small cave up ahead!"

I couldn't see the cave that she was talking about, so I had no choice to follow her and hope that she was right.

Suddenly, she fell to the ground and scrambled forward on her hands and knees.

She was right! At the bottom of the wall of solid rock was a small opening. In a flash, Summer was gone.

I didn't waste any time. I leapt forward, landing on my elbows . . . but it was too late. The T-Rex attacked, and caught my foot in his mouth.

"Ahhhhhhh!" I screamed at the top of my lungs. I was scrambling forward into the cave, trying desperately to pull my foot away from the terrible grip of the dinosaur. *"Aaaahhhhh!"*

In the darkness of the small cave, Summer grabbed my hands and pulled. I was in a dangerous tug-of-war between Summer — and a vicious, bloodthirsty dinosaur!

Suddenly, I felt my shoe slip off of my foot, and it saved my life. Only my shoe was taken — not my foot.

I pulled my leg beneath the cave, and just in time. I could see the T-Rex's huge jaws at the mouth of the cave, snapping and chewing, trying to get us.

After a few terrifying minutes, the dinosaur became frustrated. The noise outside the small cave stopped, and the ground shook as the beast thundered away to search for other forms of food. As the giant dinosaur stormed off, I leaned down, held out the camera, and snapped a picture.

"I can't believe that just happened!" Summer exclaimed. "We were attacked by a real live dinosaur!"

I knelt down, peering out the opening of the cave, making sure that the dinosaur was gone. After a few minutes, I felt it was safe to leave the shelter of the cave.

"Come on," I said. "We've got to get back through the window. It's too dangerous to stay here."

We climbed out from beneath the rock ledge and stood up. Looking around, it was still hard to believe where we were.

"Nobody is going to believe us," Summer whispered, her head turning as her eyes scanned the trees and sky.

"Yes, they will," I said, holding out my camera. "Here's the proof right here. Come on. Let's get back through the window."

Thankfully, we weren't far from the window through time. From where I stood, I could see the strange glistening window through the trees.

We crept cautiously toward it, wary of any dinosaurs that might be around.

We were almost to the window when Summer

suddenly stopped in her tracks.

"Look!" she cried out, pointing at the ground. I stopped and turned, looking to see what she was pointing at.

Beneath a tree, in a clump of dried branches and leaves . . . was an egg! There was no mistaking it.

"It's a dinosaur egg!" I said excitedly. "It's a *real* dinosaur egg!"

I snapped my head around to make sure there weren't any dinosaurs around, then sprinted to the large, oval object.

It was an egg, all right. It was just a bit bigger than a bowling ball, and shaped almost like a chicken egg, only a bit rounder. It was a dirty gray color.

I kneeled to the ground and touched the egg with my finger. It was smooth and warm. Then I reached both hands around it and picked it up.

"What are you going to do with that?" she asked, her voice filled with apprehension. She already knew what I had in mind, and I don't think she liked the idea.

"Just in case the pictures don't turn out," I said, "this will be our proof. We'll have a real dinosaur egg to show everyone. This will prove that we traveled back through time."

I could tell Summer didn't like the idea, but she

didn't say anything more. Besides . . . I was going to return to the future with the dinosaur egg whether Summer liked it or not.

And that's how this whole mess got started. Two worlds were about to collide . . . bringing a panic and terror that the city of Detroit had never before known.

Getting back through the time window was easy enough. Getting the dinosaur egg home was difficult, but I managed.

Getting people to believe me was the problem.

I called my friend, Mike Parker. He just laughed. I called the Cranbrook Institute of Science and told them I had traveled back in time and had pictures of real dinosaurs, and they said I was a kook! They said that if I called them again, they were going to call the police.

I developed the pictures at one of those on-hour photo developing places at the department store. I kept my fingers crossed for the whole hour.

Please turn out, I thought. *Please turn out. Man . . . I hope the pictures turn out good.*

They did.

They were spectacular! The picture of the Triceratops was awesome! Even the picture of the T-Rex came out bright and clear!

I had it! I had proof! I couldn't wait to show my pictures to the world.

I peddled my bike to the newspaper offices. At the front desk, I showed my pictures to a woman who picked them up, looked at them, and handed them back to me, uninterested.

"Very good fakes," she said, walking away.

"Fakes?!?!?" I cried out. "What are you talking about?!?!? These are pictures of *real* dinosaurs! My friend Summer and I traveled back in time millions of years and —"

"Look," the woman said sharply. "We don't have time for this. We are a very busy newspaper here. We report news that is true and real. Not pictures that have obviously been doctored-up by a kid with a computer."

"Doctored-up!" I cried. "These aren't

doctored-up!"

"You kids can do anything with computers these days," the woman said. Her voice was tense, and I could tell she was growing impatient with me. "You probably took pictures of plastic toy dinosaurs and made them bigger in your computer," she said.

"But I have an egg!" I exclaimed. "I have a real dinosaur egg that I brought back. I can show it to you!"

"Well, in that case, just bring the egg in here," the woman said. She picked up a piece of paper and began reading it to herself, while she continued to speak to me. "Just bring in your little dinosaur egg and we'll have a look." She looked up from the paper, glaring at me. "By the way," she said with a wink, "you don't happen to have any pictures of the abominable snowman, too, do you?"

She was making fun of me!

Well, I was going to show her! I would simply go home, retrieve the dinosaur egg, and bring it back to show her. Then she'd have to believe me.

I left the newspaper office without even saying good-bye. I peddled my bike furiously home, whizzing past yards and down side streets.

I'll show her, I thought. *I'll show everyone. I've got a real dinosaur egg, and I'm going to prove it. Maybe*

Summer and I will even be on TV! We'll be heroes!

I had placed the egg in a cardboard box and slid it beneath my bed. The last thing I wanted was my little sister to find it. Or anyone else, for that matter.

But when I walked into my house, I got the surprise of my life!

Our home was ransacked! A table was overturned, and a magazine rack had been knocked over! What was going on?!?!? What had happened?!?!?

A sudden shuffling noise came from my bedroom, and I froze.

Had we been robbed? Was the robber . . . or robbers . . . still in the house? What if somehow, someone knew about my dinosaur egg? What if someone had stolen it?!?!?

I didn't know what to do. Call the police? Run for help?

Suddenly, a strange screech came from my bedroom, followed by a ferocious chewing sound.

Oh no!

It couldn't have happened, could it? Had the dinosaur egg hatched? It seemed impossible!

Another screech came from my bedroom, then it stopped. No other sounds were heard.

Quietly, cautiously, I crept down the hall. The entire house was a mess. There was junk strewn all over the place . . . and my bedroom was the worst.

I leaned forward and peered into my room. A bookshelf had been knocked over, and there were books piled up all over the floor. My boom-box had fallen from my dresser, and it had smashed down onto my CD rack. My CD rack had broken, scattering CD's and jewel cases all over the rug.

I flopped on my stomach and peered under my bed, and a wave of terror hit me like a tidal wave.

Beneath my bed, the cardboard box lay in pieces. It had bite marks all over it! Pieces of the egg lay cracked and broken all over the floor! The dinosaur had hatched!

I stood up, looked down, and gasped.

At the floor beneath my window, just to the right of my dresser, was a hole! There were bite marks all over the wall around the hole and pieces of the wall had tumbled to the floor.

The dinosaur had chewed through my bedroom wall!

I dropped to my knees and looked out the hole, searching for the dinosaur. My eyes darted back and forth, across the yard, behind trees and shrubs, across the street.

Nothing. All I could see was green grass, trees,

and my neighbor's houses.

And for the first time, the realization of what I had done began to creep through me. The horror spread slowly at first, then built up speed like a charging rhino.

I had brought a dinosaur egg back through time. The creature had hatched. It had actually hatched in a cardboard box in my bedroom.

Worst of all, the dinosaur was loose. He was loose, and he had ripped apart my bedroom and half the house.

The real trouble was about to begin.

Also by Johnathan Rand:

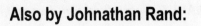

ABOUT THE AUTHOR

Johnathan Rand is the author of more than 50 books, with well over 2 million copies in print. Series include **AMERICAN CHILLERS, MICHIGAN CHILLERS, FREDDIE FERNORTNER, FEARLESS FIRST GRADER,** and **THE ADVENTURE CLUB.** He's also co-authored a novel for teens (with Christopher Knight) entitled **PANDEMIA.** When not traveling, Rand lives in northern Michigan with his wife and two dogs. He is also the only author in the world to have a store that sells only his works: **CHILLERMANIA!** is located in Indian River, Michigan. Johnathan Rand is not always at the store, but he has been known to drop by frequently. Find out more at:

www.americanchillers.com

Johnathan Rand travels internationally
for school visits and book signings! For
booking information, call:

1 (231) 238-0338!

www.americanchillers.com

Join the official

AMERICAN
CHILLERS

FAN CLUB!

Visit www.americanchillers.com for details!

All AudioCraft books are proudly printed, bound, and manufactured in the United States of America, utilizing American resources, labor, and materials.

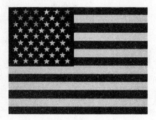

USA